Art in Nature

Tove Jansson

Art in Nature

Tove Jansson

Translated from the Swedish by
Thomas Teal

For Pentti

Art in Nature © Tove Jansson 1978
First published as *Dockskåpet* by Schildts Förlags Ab, Finland.
English translation © Thomas Teal and Sort Of Books 2012
All rights reserved

Thanks to Sophia Jansson for her encouragement and advice.

This English translation first published in 2012 by
Sort Of Books, PO Box 18678, London NW3 2FL.

Typeset in Goudy and GillSans to a design by Henry Iles.
Printed in Italy by Legoprint.

FILI   Sort Of Books gratefully acknowledges the
              financial assistance of FILI – Finnish Literature
              Exchange

176pp.
A catalogue record for this book is available from the British
Library

Print ISBN 978-0-9563086-9-6
ePub ISBN 978-1-908745-17-0

Contents

Tuulikki Pietilä's artwork for the original Swedish publication of
Dockskåpet (Doll's House), 1978, published here as *Art in Nature*

Art in Nature

Art in Nature

THE SUMMER EXHIBITION grew very quiet when it closed in the evening and the last visitors went away. A little later, boat after boat moved off from the beach and made its way back to the village on the other side of the lake. The only member of staff who stayed overnight was the caretaker. He slept in the sauna down below the great lawn where the sculptures were set out among the trees. He was very old and had a bad back, but it had been hard to find someone who enjoyed the long, lonely evenings, and they had to have a night caretaker because of the insurance.

It was a large exhibition, entitled *Art in Nature*. Every morning the caretaker unlocked the gates and people streamed into the park. They came in cars and buses from all directions, from the interior and from the capital. They brought their children and made an outing of it. They went swimming among the waterlilies and drank coffee and wandered among the birches, the children rode the swings and had their pictures taken atop the big bronze horse. More and more people wanted to see *Art in Nature*.

The caretaker was very proud of the exhibition. All day he sat in the huge glass box for painting and graphic arts and watched hundreds of feet go by. Because of his back, he couldn't see much of their faces, but he observed their feet and made a game of figuring out who they belonged to, what the rest of the person looked like. Sometimes he'd stretch his neck and take a look to see if he'd been right, and often he was. Mostly they were women in sandals, and he could see from their toes that they weren't all that young.

Almost all the feet moved respectfully. If they were with a guide, they'd stand still for a while, all turned in the same direction, and then they'd change direction all at the same time to look at something else. The lonely feet were uncertain in the beginning, then they'd move slowly at an angle, stop, stand with legs crossed, turn around, and sometimes they'd lift one foot and scratch with it because there were lots of mosquitoes. Then they'd move on, walking rather quickly along the last wall. The caretaker saw lots of feet with sturdy shoes. They'd often stand quite still, then walk along without pausing and then stand still again for quite a long time. He never looked to see what old shoes looked like higher up. Old people's shoes pointed outward, young people's inward, and children ran parallel. All of it amused him. One day two old shoes and a cane stopped beside him. He could see that she was very tired.

"Do you know," she asked, "do you know what number thirty-four is supposed to be? It looks like a package wrapped with string. Are we supposed to open it, or what?"

"I don't think so," the caretaker said. "The guide said it was a foreigner who started doing this kind of art and then kept on. . . wrapping sculptures and then finally a whole mountain. Maybe in Arizona."

"Is there a chair?" the old woman asked. "This is such a big exhibition."

He made room for her on the bench beside him and they sat next to each other for a while.

"What I admire", she said, "is that they come up with so many ideas and then they manage to carry them out and believe so strongly in what they do. I'll come back another day and look at the sculpture. You can't take in an exhibition like this one all at once; you have to take it very slowly."

The caretaker said he liked the sculptures best.

They grew up out of the grass, huge dark monuments in smooth incomprehensible formlessness or in tangled convulsions, challenging and disturbing. They stood everywhere among the birches as if they'd sprung up from the soil, and when the summer night arrived and the mist drifted in from the lake they were as beautiful as granite crags or withered trees.

Each evening, he would close the gates and continue along the shoreline to put out the fire in the sausage grill and see to it that everything was as it should be. He'd replace the moss that children had pulled off the big rocks, and he'd collect the coins from the wishing well and lay them out on a newspaper to dry. He'd check to make sure none of the ashtrays were burning, then empty them carefully into the open, sculptural oven. The June nights were quiet and the lake motionless, with a mirror image beneath each little island. The guard loved his repeated evening strolls, closing for the night. At the gate there was a smell of hay and fertilizer from the farms all around. Along the shore was the smell of mud and grass, then the sauna with its smell of wet soot, and when he walked by the sculptures made of plaster he could smell tar. All of them were impregnated with tar to protect them from the rain. He'd helped to paint them himself. During the day, he didn't notice the smells; he heard only voices and feet. The caretaker liked the evenings and the nights. He didn't need much sleep and often sat by himself in the peace and quiet of the lake shore for hours. He didn't remember, he didn't worry, he just was. The only thing that troubled him was that the exhibition would close in the autumn. He'd grown used to it and couldn't imagine another kind of life.

One evening he was making his rounds of the area as usual. He had closed the gates, and everything should have been shipshape. Then he smelled smoke, smoke from something burning. He was beside himself. Fire. Something was on fire! Half stumbling, he tried to run, a few steps in one direction, a few in another, until he realized that the smoke was only coming from the sausage grill. Intruders had hidden somewhere on the property and had now begun grilling sausages down by the lake. Relief made him furious. He headed off across the lawn down towards the shoreline as fast as he could go, but he tried to walk quietly. Soon he heard voices, a man's and a woman's, and they were quarrelling. The caretaker snuck closer and looked at them. They were middle-aged adults who should have known better than to break the exhibition rules. The man looked pale. He was wearing an American shirt and had a salmon fly in his hat. The woman was rather fat and wearing an outfit printed with little flowers. They were grilling sausages and drinking beer, and they were arguing. The guard listened for a while. It was a perfectly ordinary domestic quarrel. Then he strode forward, struck the ground with his cane and shouted, "This is outrageous! You can't have a fire here after closing. It's absolutely forbidden! When we're closed, we're closed. What are you doing here?"

"Good heavens," the woman said. "Albert, I told you we shouldn't."

The man jumped up and was going to pour lake water on the grill, but the caretaker yelled, "Stop that! You'll crack the grill. It has to burn out by itself!" Suddenly he was very tired and sat down on a rock. The man and the woman were silent.

"Responsibility," the caretaker said. "Does the word mean anything to you? Do you know what it means? Every night I'm responsible for this whole enormous exhibition, and for the woods, as well. There are works of art here by the country's finest artists, and it's all on my shoulders."

"Svea," the man said, "give him a sausage and a glass of beer." But the caretaker turned it down. He didn't want to be placated. The evening had faded into a summer night, and a light mist came gliding in over the lake and hid the islands. The trunks of the birch trees grew whiter.

"Perhaps I should introduce myself," the man said. "Fagerlund."

"Räsänen," said the guard.

The woman started packing up her baskets. Clearly they couldn't go on eating and drinking.

"And what is that?" Räsänen asked, pointing his cane at a brown parcel they had put down on a rock. The woman explained quickly that it was a work of art they had picked out and paid for. It was the first painting they had ever purchased and so of course they had to celebrate. "It's a silkscreen," she said.

"That's no excuse," Räsänen said. "Anyway, the correct name is serigraph. They make lots and lots of copies, but it counts as art anyway. What's it of?"

"It's abstract," Fagerlund said. "But we think it's two chairs turned a little away from each other."

Räsänen said that he couldn't recall any such chairs, and then the wife said it had been furthest in on the right, two perfectly ordinary kitchen chairs in front of some wallpaper. She spoke eagerly and it was clear she was trying to ingratiate herself.

"You're wrong," her husband said. "They're folding chairs, the kind you can whisk out of the way in a second. And anyway, they're not important. It's the background that's important." He turned to Räsänen and said, "You see, it opens out. You can see life going on outside. It could be a big city. It's certainly not kitchen wallpaper!"

His wife laughed and said, "You and your big ideas. It's wallpaper – anyone can see that. Don't be an ass. They were sitting in their chairs and now they've gone and they kicked the chairs apart as they left. Maybe they quarrelled. What do you think? Did they quarrel?"

"They probably just got tired," Fagerlund said. "They got sick and tired and went out."

"Yes, of course," she said. "One of them went to the bar around the corner."

Räsänen waited a while and then he said how it's funny about art. Each person sees what he sees, and that's the whole idea. But why hadn't they bought something prettier and easier – a landscape, for example?

They didn't answer. The wife had turned away towards the lake and she was wiping her eyes and blowing her nose.

The caretaker said, "Or you could do this. Since a piece of art can be just about anything, and since we only see what we want to see, you could just not unwrap it and hang the package on the wall. Then you won't need to argue." He poked the coals with his cane. The fire was almost out.

After a while she said, "How do you mean, the package?"

"I mean with the paper and the string and everything. You saw some picture packages like that in the exhibition, that's one of the things they do these days. Maybe you should just imagine what's inside, and then imagine different things."

She looked around at him and said, "Are you being serious?"

Fagerlund said, "Svea, Herr Räsänen is teasing you. We should go."

She turned and started grumpily gathering up their baskets and sweaters and all the rest of their things.

"Wait a minute," the caretaker said. "I'm perfectly serious. It occurred to me just now. You just need to make the wrapping a little prettier, use more string, you know, fishing line or shoemaker's thread. Lots of string. I've seen how it should look." He drew a picture in the sand with his cane. "Like this and this. Very carefully. And cover it with glass."

"But that was expensive!" she burst out. "Anyone could make a package like you're talking about at home and just hang it up on the wall!"

"No," said the caretaker. "I don't think they could. Because then there's nothing mysterious about it." He was happy, almost elated at finally grasping the point of the wrapped art. "Now you can go home," he said. "You'll have to climb over the gate, because I don't fancy walking all the way back to unlock it."

"Albert," she said, "you'll have to carry the package." She gave it a look as if it were about to burst into flames.

Fagerlund picked up the package and put it down again. "No," he said. "We'll unwrap it here and now. We'll let Herr Räsänen decide what it's a picture of."

Then she shouted, "Stop that!" and started to cry in earnest and said she didn't want to know, she just wanted to see it her own way and not be intimidated.

The caretaker was silent for a moment, then he said, "It's too dark. We couldn't see anything anyway." He stood up and said goodbye to his guests. When they'd gone, he sat down again and watched the grill for a while, then he walked slowly back among the sculptures, which now, at the darkest hour of the summer night, were nothing but shadows with clearly defined shapes. But what I said was completely right, he thought. It's the mystery that's important, somehow very important. He went and lay down in the sauna with its four bare walls. It was nice to look at them and fall asleep without all the humdrum thoughts he was used to.

The Monkey

THE NEWSPAPER CAME at five o'clock, as it did every morning. He switched on the lamp by his bed, got into his slippers, and shuffled very slowly across the slippery cement floor, taking his usual route among the modelling stands, their shadows black as holes. He'd polished the floor after the last plaster casting. The wind was blowing, and the streetlight outside his studio made the shadows swing, driving them apart and pulling them together again. It was like walking through woods in a moonlit storm. He liked it. The monkey was awake in her cage, hanging on the bars, whining ingratiatingly.

"Bloody monkey," said the sculptor and went out into the front hall to pick up his paper. On his way back to bed he opened the cage door and the monkey ran up his arm and clung firmly to his shoulder. She was shivering. He put on her collar and attached the leash to his wrist. The monkey was an ordinary guenon from Tangier that someone had bought cheap and sold dear. Every now and then she came down with pneumonia and needed penicillin. The kids in the neighbourhood knitted sweaters for her.

He got back into bed and opened his paper. The monkey lay quietly warming herself with her arms around his neck. After a while, she sat down in front of him, her pretty hands crossed over her stomach, and stared steadily into his eyes, an expression of perpetual, sad patience on her narrow grey face. "Stare away, you damned orangutan," the sculptor said and went on reading. At the second or third page, the monkey would suddenly and with lightning precision jump through the newspaper, but always through the pages he'd already read. It was a ritual – the paper was ripped to shreds, the monkey shrieked in triumph and then lay down to sleep. It could be liberating every morning at five o'clock to read through all the world's worst shit and then have the shittiness confirmed by seeing it all shredded and rendered unreadable. She helped him dispose of it. Now she jumped. "You bugger," said the sculptor. "You cretinous old flea circus!" He invented new insults every morning. He stuffed her in under the quilt to sleep and made sure she had air.

The monkey began to snore and he turned to the arts column. He knew they'd pan his new show, but he found instead a patronizing generosity that he hadn't expected. He was so old they had to be kind. Without the monkey, he'd have turned to the arts column at once, but she helped him to read it in passing as if it were just another page. "Sleep, you little bastard," he said. "You're too dumb to understand. All you care about is getting attention. And breaking things." It was true: the monkey was like all the rest of them. The tiniest crack, the least stain or defect and her fingers were there to make it worse and pick it apart. She noticed everything, every tiny sign of weakness, and that's where she'd bite and rip and tear. That's the way monkeys are, but they don't know any better and so we forgive them. The others are unforgivable.

The sculptor dropped the newspaper on the floor and turned towards the wall. When he woke up, it was much too late and he got out of bed with the usual awful feeling of having wasted time. He was very tired. First he put the monkey in her cage. She didn't move, just sat in one corner, her back very narrow in its hand-knit sweater. There was heavy traffic on the street outside, and the elevator was running nonstop. He rinsed out some clay rags and swept the floor. It's easy to sweep polished cement, a long brush that gets in between the legs of the modelling stands and glides across the floor like silk, then into the dustpan and into the trash. He liked sweeping.

Out of habit, he went to the window a couple of times, but he could no longer see out because it was covered with plastic to soften the light. He fed the monkey. He decided to change his sheets and considered dragging the plaster box out into the courtyard but decided against it and did a little more sweeping instead. He collected some old scraps of soap too small to get a grip on, dropped them into a jar and poured in water. He took the clay rags from the statuette and looked at it, swung the top of the modelling stand halfway round and back again. He walked over to the monkey cage and said, "You old carcass, you're so ugly you make me sick." The monkey screamed a challenge and stuck her hands out through the bars.

He called Savolainen, but hung up before anyone answered. For that matter, he might as well go eat and get it over with. He decided to take the monkey with him to give her a little change of scenery. But she didn't want to go, just threw herself back and forth from one side of the cage to the other. "Okay, what do you want?" he said. "Do you want to come out, or do you want to stay here in this mess?" He waited. Finally she came out and sat quite still while he put on her catskin coat. When he tied her cap under her chin, she raised her face and looked at him, a straight, expressionless gaze from yellow eyes placed close together. The sculptor looked away, suddenly upset by the unmoving animal's attitude of absolute indifference.

They went out together and he held her inside his coat. The wind was still blowing. Some youngsters were hanging around on the esplanade, and when they caught sight of him they came running, shouting, "It's the monkey! It's the monkey!" She jumped out of his coat and rushed back and forth on her leash, screaming at the boys, who hollered back and followed the two of them to the corner. There she bit one of them, a quick, sharp bite. "Shitty monkey! Shitty monkey!" the children chanted. He hurried into the café and put the monkey on the floor.

"So you brought it back again," said the doorman. "You know what happened last time. Animals aren't allowed."

"Animals?" the sculptor said. "Do you mean cats and dogs? Or are you referring to your customers and the way they behave?"

Savolainen and the others were sitting at a table eating.

"Monkeys", Savolainen observed, "are known for their destructiveness."

"What the fuck are you talking about?"

"Their need to destroy. They break things."

"And for their tenderness," the sculptor said. "They try to offer comfort."

Lindholm grinned. "I'll bet you could use some of that today. But it could've been worse."

The monkey sat inside his coat; he could feel her shivering.

"Worse?" Savolainen burst out with mock horror. "Do you mean, *even* worse?"

"Take it easy, you little bastard," said the sculptor, and then, in the sudden silence, "I was talking to the monkey."

"Listen," Pehrman said. "You shouldn't care what they say. They write what they think, and so what? Except it's a shame everyone believes what they say. We're *out*, that's all. Back at the bottom. And it'll be hell to crawl back up again."

"If you're old," Stenberg pointed out. "What does it eat? Clay? Sure looks like it. What do you call it?"

"Bloody shitboot," he said. "Sadistic fucking birdbrain."

All at once the monkey ran across the table, knocking over glasses as she went, bit Stenberg right through the ear and then ran screeching back to hide in his coat.

"Tenderness," said Lindholm. "Wasn't that what you said? A very tender-hearted animal."

The sculptor stood up and replied that that was just exactly what he'd said and moreover he didn't care for the menu at this place and he had things to do.

"There's a Tarzan film at the Ritz," said the doorman. "I assume that's where you're headed."

"Of course," the sculptor said. "How intelligent you are." He overtipped him out of pure contempt.

The wind had picked up. They walked across the esplanade; the boys had gone. It's no use, the sculptor thought. There's nothing in it for me any more. The monkey was having a fit. He tried to make it warm for her under his coat, but she wiggled her way out and was choking on her own collar. She started to scream, so finally he undid her leash. For a moment she didn't move, then she jumped out of his hands and up into a tree, held tight to the trunk and hung there like a little grey rat, looking scared. She was shivering with the cold. Her long tail was within his reach – he could have caught her, but he just stood there and did nothing. Then, quick as lightning, the monkey disappeared up into the leafless tree and hung from one of the highest limbs like some dark fruit, and he thought, You poor little bastard. You're freezing, but you've got to climb.

The Cartoonist

THE NEWSPAPER HAD BEEN running Blubby for almost twenty years when Allington quit and they were forced to continue the strip with a different artist. They had material for only a couple of weeks ahead, so the need was urgent. They had contractual agreements with other countries that promised a security margin of at least two months. And Blubby was a clever strip that tore along at a furious pace, so not just anyone could do it. They took a handful of artists on approval and gave them office space, which saved time on supervision. The same assignment for all of them, obviously. They dismissed two of them after only a few days and replaced them with others. The editor in charge went around a couple of times a day to have a look and help them get a handle on what the paper was after. He was a tall man by the name of Fried. He had a bad back, presumably because he was forever leaning down over cartoonists' drawing boards. There was one ambitious young artist who seemed to be the best of them, but he wasn't good enough yet.

"You have to remember," Fried said, "you have to keep in mind the whole time that the tension has to mount. You've got a strip of three or four panels, five if absolutely necessary, but four's better. Okay. In the first one, you resolve the tension from the previous day. Catharsis, relief, the drama continues. You build up new tension in the second panel, increase it in panel three, and so on. I've explained that. You're good, but you get lost in details, commentary, embroidery that gets in the way of the red thread. It has to be a straight line, simple, and move towards a peak, a climax, you see?"

"I know," said Samuel Stein. "I know. I'm trying."

"Imagine someone opening his newspaper," Fried went on. "He's sleepy, he's in a lousy mood, he's in a hurry to get to work. He checks the headlines on page one and dives into the comics. He's in no condition to grasp subtleties right at the moment, that's too much to ask. But his curiosity needs a little excitement, and he wants a laugh, wants to grin at something funny for a second – natural enough, right? Okay, he gets all that. We give it to him. It's important. Do you see what I'm saying?"

"Yes," Stein said. "I think I got it from the beginning. It's just that it all has to happen so quickly. I just don't have the space to get everything in and still do something good – not really."

"It'll be good," Fried said. "You'll get there. Relax. I can tell you confidentially that you're one of the better ones. You draw well, and your backgrounds are fine. I have to move on."

It was a very small room with brown walls, essentially just a storeroom weighed down with crowded shelves and cupboards and a large, heavy, old-fashioned desk that had drawers all the way to the floor. The walls were covered with old calendars, clippings, ads, odd posters, announcements, clumps of paper, all held in place by thumbtacks. The room gave an impression of a life that had passed long ago and been forgotten, a life no one had had time to tidy away. Samuel Stein liked the room. It gave him a feeling of being hidden and safe along with his work. And he liked being a cog in the machinery of the great, distinguished newspaper, liked feeling its respect.

The room was very cold. He stood up, and the chill engulfed him. The whole time he could hear the distant thudding of the printing presses and, over them, the sound of traffic on the street. He was freezing. A work blouse and a sweater hung beside the door. He put on the sweater and stuck his hands into the pockets. In the right pocket, Sam Stein found a piece of paper, a list. He read it standing at the window. "Used", it said in very small letters. "Ski skate etc. fun of government and modern art went to ball 1 masked 2 cocktail p. gangster astronaut 3x Love + vamp out hamburger India ink lighter background laundry call A.G."

It was a cartoonist who had worked here, and the sweater was his. Stein was curious and opened a drawer. It contained a mix of pencil stumps, tape, empty ink bottles, paper clips, all the usual junk. But maybe worse than usual. All of it had been stirred together as if in a rage. He opened the next drawer. It was empty, completely empty. He let the other drawers be and put on some water for tea – there was a hotplate on the floor under the window. It could have been Allington who'd had this room. Maybe he never worked at home, maybe he sat right here for twenty years and drew his Blubby. He had stopped abruptly, in the middle of a story. And you're supposed to give six months' notice. The outline had apparently got lost at the fifty-third strip. Normal length was usually eighty. Stein had asked why Allington couldn't reconstruct the story. No, he wasn't able to. Didn't he want to? Had he forgotten?

"I don't know," Fried said. "It was a different department that took care of that. Don't worry about it. Go on from where he stopped and do something of your own, but preferably so no one will see the break. You can leave off the signature."

The tea water was boiling. Stein removed the saucepan and pulled out the plug. He took down the cup and the sugar he'd found on a shelf. There was no spoon. He had his own teabags.

♦♦♦

Six days later Fried came in and said that now they'd decided. Stein had the job, no contest, and there'd be a contract in a few days. For seven years. The board had been very pleased, but wanted to re-emphasize the need for greater suspense. Fried looked tired as he stood there with a smile on his soft, vague features. He stepped forward and shook hands with Stein and touched his shoulder gently in a gesture of encouragement and protectiveness.

"That's great," Stein said. "That's really great. Can you use the stuff I've done, or should I start over from the beginning?"

"No, God no. We don't have time for that. We'll throw in the material we've got and you can push up the speed until we've got two months in the bank."

"Tell me something," Stein said. "Did he work in this room?"

"Allington?"

"Yes. Allington."

"Yes, this was his room. It's kind of fitting that you assume his mantle in the very same work room, don't you think?"

"There's a lot of his things here. I mean, I didn't poke around that much. But is he going to come and get them?"

"I'll see to it that it's all moved out," Fried said. "It's very crowded in here. I'll ask someone to get it all out of the way."

"Is he dead?" Stein said.

"No, no, not at all."

"So he got sick."

"My dear fellow, don't worry yourself," Fried replied. "He's perfectly all right. And now I will simply wish you good luck with the job."

♦♦♦

In the beginning, Stein worked without touching anything in the room. His first strip was published, without a signature, and no one noticed the difference. Anyway, Allington hadn't signed his strips for the last three years of his contract, and that helped. Stein increased his pace to several strips a day. He was learning more and more. He learned to do half a dozen strips in pencil and then ink them all at the same time, beginning with pure black surfaces in the morning. Once he was warmed up, he'd start on details and along towards afternoon when he was completely sure of his hand, he'd draw the long lines and the elegant small bits that needed to be done quickly and deftly. Then he'd go on to the next batch.

He came steadily closer to the prescribed lead time. They had congratulated him when his first strip was printed without any public reaction. He was depressed that day, but it passed, and he went on working steadily, pleased at doing a good job that was very well paid. He felt secure. He no longer had to dash around with illustrations and confer with irresolute, pretentious authors – three or four trips for every blessed dust jacket. Take orders, meet authors, turn in his work, wait, go in to collect his fee, and occasionally go up to the printer's once or twice to make sure the colour separations were correct.

Now everything went like clockwork. He didn't even have to deliver his work; he just left the day's drawings on his desk and someone picked them up that evening. He picked up his salary in the cashier's office every other week. Fried no longer paid him visits. He just saw him now and then on the stairs.

"You never come to look any more," Stein said.

"No longer necessary, my boy," said Fried jokingly. "You're doing splendidly. But God help you if you get stuck or take a wrong turn. I'll be there like a shot!"

"God forbid!" Stein said and laughed. He had bought himself an electric heater and the newspaper had paid for it. They were taking care of him now, and with good reason. Blubby ran in thirty or forty countries.

Occasionally Stein would go down around the corner and have a drink. He liked the dark, messy bar. It was full of men in the same line of work who talked about their jobs, had a drink, and went back to the paper. He met the other cartoonists. They were friendly and treated him like a greenhorn, a boy who wasn't really into the game yet but seemed quite promising. Their attitude was more affectionate than condescending. They didn't buy each other rounds; just hung over the bar for a while with a glass in one hand, then went back.

There was one of them he admired, an extremely talented artist named Carter. Carter didn't do pencil sketches, he drew directly with India ink. Terrifying, naturalistic, historical scenes. He was a heavy, very ugly man with reddish hair who moved slowly. He never smiled but seemed amused by what went on around him.

"Tell me something," he said. "Are you one of those people who are prevented from doing Great Art because they draw comic strips?"

"No," Stein said. "Not at all."

"Good for you," Carter said. "They're insufferable. They're neither fish nor fowl and they can't stop talking about it."

"Did you know Allington?" Stein asked.

"Not well."

"Was he one of them? I mean, one of the insufferable ones?"

"No."

"But why did he quit?"

"He got tired," Carter said and emptied his drink and went back to do some work.

The newspaper had forgotten to tidy up Allington's room, which was just as well. Stein liked sitting encapsulated in a century of collected and forgotten props. They made up a kind of warm quilting, a faded tapestry that surrounded him softly on all sides. Eventually he started opening drawers, one a day, the way you open windows on an advent calendar. He found the drawers with the most recent fan mail, bound in packets with rubber bands: "Answered", "Can Wait", "Important", "Send drawing of B". Another empty drawer. A drawer of glossy prints of Blubby on heavy stock, sophisticated vignettes for adults and funny pictures for children. Papers, papers, clippings, bills, socks, photos of children, receipts, cigarettes, corks, string – the whole accumulation of dead life that heaps up around people who've lost the strength to be attentive. Nothing about the strip. Stein couldn't find any notes about Allington's work other than that list in the right-hand pocket of the sweater.

As Stein worked on Blubby, Allington grew more and more real to him. Allington not coming up with ideas and staring down at the street through the grey window panes, Allington brewing tea and rooting around in his drawers, answering the phone or completely forgotten between deadlines, Allington famous and worn out. Did he feel lonely, or was he wary of people? Did he work better in the mornings or later when the paper was quiet? What did he do when he got stuck, or did he work at a steady pace for twenty years? Now I need to be careful, Sam Stein thought. I mustn't romanticize him. If Allington had stood at a machine for twenty years, no one would have made a big deal of it. He was popular, and well paid. So am I.

One weekend, Carter asked Stein if he'd like to come out to his place in the country. It was a great mark of favour; Carter disliked almost everyone and wanted to be left in peace. It was early spring, and the countryside was completely quiet. Carter took him around and showed him his pigs and chickens. He showed him his snakes, lifted a stone in the lawn very carefully and said, "There they are. They're still a little sleepy, but they'll liven up."

Stein was fascinated. "What do you feed them?" he said.

"Nothing. They feed themselves. There are lots of frogs and toads and other things they like."

Stein had heard that Carter never answered letters, that he didn't even open them. He wasn't the least bit curious about their contents, and his conscience didn't bother him.

"You can't do that," Stein said. "You're famous, they admire you. Those letters are from children, and they need to be answered."

"Why?" said Carter.

They were sitting in front of the house with drinks. It was very warm and still.

"They have faith," Stein said. "When I was little I wrote to the President of France and asked him to close down the Foreign Legion."

"And did you get an answer?"

"Certainly did. My mother wrote a reply from the President and said now they were going to shut the whole thing down. With French stamps and everything."

"You're too young," Carter said. "It's better for them to get used to it right from the start, you know, used to the fact that things don't turn out the way you imagined and that it doesn't matter that much." He went off to feed the pigs and was gone for quite a while. When he came back, Stein started talking about Allington and how he'd worked steadily for twenty years and then just walked away without even leaving an outline.

"He got tired," Carter said.

"Did he ever talk to you about it?"

"No, he said almost nothing. One day he was gone. Left a note on his desk. In fact it was a half-finished strip, and on it he'd written 'I'm tired.' He never even came back for his money."

"But didn't they try to find him?"

"Good lord," Carter said. "Just listen to you. Didn't they try to find him? Holy Moses. The entire police department was out searching. Everyone was hysterical. Blubby about to breathe his last ... The franchise holders got wind of it and were running in and out of the offices like madmen."

"Franchise holders?"

"You don't know a thing, do you?" said Carter, lighting his pipe. "The people who live on Blubby. Have you never seen a charming little Blubby in plastic or marzipan or candle wax?" He stood up and started walking slowly back and forth on the grass, chanting, "Blubby curtains, Blubby jelly, Blubby clocks and Blubby socks, Blubby shirts and Blubby shorts ... Shall I go on?"

"I'd rather you didn't," Stein said.

"I could go on for an hour. Allington made sketches for all of it. He was very careful with his comic strip. He was very particular; everything had to be just so. You know, he supervised all of it down to the tiniest detail. Textiles, metals, paper products, rubber, wood, all of it ... And then there were the Blubby films and Blubby Week and children's theatre and journalists and dissertations about Blubby and all the charities and something called the Blubby Marmalade Campaign ... Holy Moses. Anyway, he couldn't ever say no. And then he got tired."

Stein said nothing, but he looked frightened.

"Don't worry," Carter went on. "None of it's your headache. All you have to do is draw and the paper will take care of all the rest of it."

"But how do you know all that?" Stein said. "He didn't talk to people."

"I've got eyes in my head," Carter said. "And I draw my own strip. But, you see, I can say no. And it's no skin off my nose if they mess around with my work. Do you get a lot of letters?"

"Yes," Stein said. "But they're all to him. Fried told me to give them to the department. They've got a stamp with Allington's signature and they've got people who sit there and answer them. And if I'm going to write letters," Stein went on angrily, "I'll sign my own name to them, not someone else's."

"You're awfully careful with your name, aren't you?" said Carter with a grin.

They said no more about Allington. Stein had meant to ask if he'd ever been found, but he felt suddenly dejected and said nothing.

Later they saw one another in the bar from time to time, in passing.

Sam Stein came to his third outline. He would work them up in pencil sketches with a little dialogue and give them to Fried. Five or six days later, they'd come back with corrections and he'd find them on his desk. "Better, but you need to pick up the pace." "Cut the references to toilet paper and cemeteries." "Numbers sixty-five to seventy too subtle." "No jokes about the government and the manufacturers." And so on.

People at the paper started to recognize him; he began to belong. It was mostly Johnson he talked to in the bar. Johnson was in advertising, and sometimes when he had the time he'd answer Allington's fan mail.

"Oh, Carter," said Johnson. "I know. All he cares about are his pigs and those snakes – and money. He's so fabulously talented, the drawings run out of him like diarrhea, but he has absolutely no ambition. And why should he? Did you know he also grows vegetables and some cousin of his sells them at a farmers' market?"

"He never answers fan mail," Stein said. "He doesn't give a damn. You know what? These cartoonists – either they're all touchy and conscience-stricken or else they don't give a damn about anything. Am I right?"

"Maybe you're right and maybe you're wrong. I don't know if they're all nuts to begin with or if they get that way from drawing comic strips. Shall we have another?" It was evening and they were lingering in the bar. It was really too late to go back and get anything done.

"This thing with Allington," Stein said. "I can't get free of him. He's everywhere. What actually happened?"

"He went nuts," Johnson said.

"You mean, really?"

"Well, sort of, more or less."

Sam Stein leaned over the bar and looked into the mirror behind the bottles. I look tired, he thought. But in a few weeks, I can take it easier. I could have Blubby go to a bar. It's been a long time since he did that. He'd gone through four years of Allington's old strips. No one remembered further back than that.

He said, "Is there anyone who knows where he is? I want to talk to him."

"Why? You're doing fine."

"That's not it. I want to know why he couldn't go on."

"But you know that," said Johnson amiably. "You've already figured it out. It's like drummers in jazz bands. After a certain number of years, it's just over. What do you say? Shall we have another?"

"No," Stein said. "I don't think so. I thought I'd do some laundry this evening."

♦♦♦

The next morning, Stein went into the storage room behind Allington's office and started pulling down cartons from the shelves, bundles of letters, bags, and boxes. He lined them up on the floor in order to go through all of it. There was fan mail in four boxes and a suitcase. On three of them was the word "Done". One said "Sent things", and on the suitcase was written "Pathetic Cases." On yet another little box Allington had written "Good Letters" and on another, "Anonymous." Product samples, Blubby in every possible material and packaging, all of them with wide blue eyes with big black pupils. Outlines crossed out with a felt-tip pen, all except one, something about the Wild West. A notation: "Not used".

Stein smoothed out Allington's manuscript and put it on his desk. Maybe he could use it. The next carton was "Unsorted" and it broke when he pulled it out and a sea of paper flowed out across the floor. Poor man, Stein thought. How he must have hated paper. Messages, queries, bills, exhortations, pleas, accusations, declarations of love ... There was an address book with neatly noted names and in parentheses the wife's name or the husband's, names of the children, of the dog, or the cat ... Maybe the courtesy of remembering made letters a little shorter for him – it got him off the hook more easily.

Suddenly Stein didn't want to know more. All he wanted was to try and find Allington. He needed to understand. He had a seven-year contract and he needed to be calmed or alarmed, one or the other, but he had to know.

The next day Stein tried to find Allington's address, but no one could help him.

"My dear boy," Fried said, "you're just wasting your time. Allington has no address. His apartment was essentially untouched and he never came back."

"But the police," Stein said. "They searched for him. They did a lousy job. Here's his address book. A thousand names or more. Have they seen it?"

"Of course they have. They called a few people, but no one knew anything. What do you want with him?"

"I don't know exactly. I want to talk to him."

"I'm sorry," Fried said, "but we've got better things to do. He left us in the lurch, and now we've fixed it. You need to stop brooding about Allington."

◆◆◆

That same evening the boy appeared, a kid six or seven years old. Stein had put his work away and was ready to leave.

"It was hard to find you," the child said. "I've brought you a present."

It was a large flat package, wrapped with lots of pieces of string. When Stein had untied them all, he found inside a new package tightly circled with tape. The boy stood quietly as he cut and tore it, until he reached yet another package, which was bound together with plastic bands.

"This is getting more and more exciting," Stein said. "It's like a treasure hunt!" The boy was solemn and silent. The packages grew smaller and smaller, but each wrapping was as hard to open as the one before. Sam Stein began to be uneasy. He wasn't used to children and it bothered him pretending to be Allington. Finally he came to the end and opened a Blubby drawn on silver paper and wearing an astronaut's spacesuit. He blurted out admiring comments that were much too exaggerated. The child didn't move a muscle.

"But what's your name?" Stein said and knew at once that it was the wrong question, utterly and completely wrong.

The boy said nothing. Then, in a hostile tone, "Where have you been?"

"I was on a trip," Stein said quickly. "A long trip to a foreign country."

It sounded idiotic. The boy looked at him very quickly and looked away again.

"Do you draw a lot?" Stein asked.

"No."

It was awful, totally hopeless. His eyes wandered across the cluttered room looking for help, something to say to this child who admired Allington. He picked up the Wild West from his desk and said, "This one isn't done yet. I don't really know how to go on. Come and have a look."

The boy came closer.

"You see, Blubby's in the Wild West," he said, feeling suddenly relieved. "The bad guys are trying to take his spring, which is his only source of water. They've hired a lawyer, and the lawyer has come up with a wicked plan. He's going to say that the spring doesn't belong to Blubby at all. It's owned by the state."

"Shoot him," the boy said calmly.

"Yes, maybe you're right. On the street or in a bar?"

"No. That's too ordinary. Have them ride after each other and the lawyer shoots first."

"Good," Stein said. "It's important that he shoots first, so he's had his chance. So it's okay if he dies."

The boy looked at him and eventually said, "Your new place is too far away for me. When are you coming to mine? I made an altar for you, with pictures."

"How nice," Stein said. "Maybe I will soon. I've got so much work to do right now. Have you ever drawn with India ink?"

"No."

"Give it a try. Write your address and my address. Side by side."

"But you already know them."

"Yes, but write them anyway. Names and all."

The boy wrote, slowly and neatly.

When he'd gone, Samuel Stein returned all of John Allington's things to the back room. They were the possessions of a dead man. But he had the address now of the Allington who was alive.

◆◆◆

Allington was living in a hotel in a suburb. He was middle-aged, a perfectly ordinary man, one of the invisible people on a bus. Dressed in something grayish brown. Stein introduced himself and explained that he was his replacement for the comic strip.

"Come in," Allington said. "We can have a drink." The room was clean and seemed very empty.

"How's it going?" Allington asked.

"Quite well. I'm on my fourth outline."

"And how's Fried?"

"There's his bad back, of course, but otherwise he's fine."

"Funny," Allington said. "All of that was so important. How long is your contract?"

"Seven years."

"Sounds right. They don't want to drag it out longer when the strip's been running for such a long time. Sooner or later, people are going to want something new." Allington went out to the kitchen to get their drinks. When he came back, he asked how Stein had found his address.

"There was a boy, Bill Harvey. He came in with a drawing for you. For that matter, here it is."

Allington looked at Blubby the astronaut. "I know," he said. "He was one of the hardest to answer. Never stopped writing. Did he believe you were me?"

"I don't know. I'm not sure I pulled it off."

"Do you get your mail directly or does it go to Johnson?"

"To Johnson."

"That's better."

"One thing," Stein said. "It doesn't feel good pretending to be someone I'm not. I'm not used to it."

"I understand," Allington said. "But you get into the swing of it and it gets to be just another part of the game. You spit out letters faster and faster and they take them at face value. You anticipate their reactions and accept their inexhaustible silliness. The same ideas over and over again. With stupid variations."

"Nevertheless," said Stein carefully, "it's a question of responsibility, isn't it? I mean, all these people open their newspapers and read the comics.They read them and they're influenced. Maybe they're not aware of it, but they can't help themselves. You could sneak in a whole lot of stuff that was ..." He paused. "Positive, somehow. Teach them something. Or comfort them. Or scare them – make them think. Do you know what I mean?"

"I know," Allington said. "I did that sort of thing for four or five years."

They were silent for a moment.

"We never found your last outline," Stein said. "Did it get lost?"

"Probably."

"But I found one about the Wild West. I was thinking of using it. Shame to waste it."

"The usual story?"

"More or less. Only sixty strips. Maybe a few more."

"Well, well," Allington said. "I think it was something they turned down. You can only use the Wild West maybe once a year. But put it in with the rest; it won't matter. Where do you work?"

"In your room."

"Is it still just as cold?"

"I've put in an electric heater." Stein was quiet for a moment and then asked what he should do with all the stuff in the closet and the desk drawers.

"Have someone carry it out in the yard."

"But I can't do that," Stein said. "After all, it's a life. You can't just dump it in the yard."

Allington started to laugh, and his face was suddenly very appealing. "Stein," he said, "not a life. A little piece of a life. See, I'm not done yet. What is it that bothers you? That I quit and just walked away from all of it? You've only got seven years. You'll get through it somehow. You're not going to hang yourself." He filled their glasses and said, "There was one who did. A villa on the Riviera and a yacht and all the rest of it, and then he goes and hangs himself. Maybe it's not that unusual, but he wrote a letter to other cartoonists and warned them against long contracts. They've got the letter at the paper in their secret museum. Do you want ice?"

"No thanks," Stein said. "I take it straight. What shall I do with this kid? Bill."

"Nothing. He'll grow up and start to admire something else. Believe me, it doesn't pay to go soft in this game."

"You're one to talk," Stein said. "I've looked in your drawers."

"And what did you think?"

Stein hesitated. Then he said, "That you got very tired."

Allington stood up and walked to the window. It was getting dark. He made a movement as if to draw the curtains but then let them be. He stood looking down at the street.

"I think I should be going," Stein said. "Thought I'd go back and work for a while."

"It was their eyes," said Allington without turning around. "Their cartoon eyes. The same stupid round eyes all the time. Amazement, terror, delight, and so on – all you have to do is move the pupil and an eyebrow here and there and people think you're brilliant. Just imagine achieving so much with so little. And in fact, they always look exactly the same. But they have to do new things all the time. All the time. You know that. You've learned that, right?" His voice was quiet, but it sounded as if he were speaking through clenched teeth. He went on without waiting for a reply. "Novelty! Always something new. You start searching for ideas. Among the people you know, among your friends. Your own head is a blank, so you start using everything they've got, squeezing it dry, and no matter what people tell you, all you can think is, Can I use it?" Allington swung around and stared at Stein, suddenly silent, the ice cubes tinkling violently in his glass. His hand had started shaking. Slowly he said, "Do you understand? Do you see that you can't afford it, that you don't have time to be in a hurry?"

Sam Stein had risen from his chair.

"Every day," Allington went on, "every week and month and year and new year and it never ends – the same creatures with the same pupils creeping around you and over you and never stopping ..." Allington's face was changed, swollen, and a muscle was twitching by his mouth.

Stein looked away.

"Forgive me," said John Allington. "I didn't mean to ... Mostly things are fine. In fact they're getting better and better. I've been doing well recently. They tell me I'm much improved. Sit down. Let's sit for a while. Do you like evening?"

"No," Stein said. "No. I don't like it."

"Do you ever see Johnson?"

"Yes, in the bar sometimes. I like him."

"Collects stamps. But only with boats on them. I heard about a man who collected stamps with musical instruments. Funny about collectors. I'm interested in mosses. You know, moss. But then I'd have to live in the country."

"They grow very slowly," Stein said. "And then, as you say, you have to live in the country. And they say the birds destroy them if they have a bad year."

He stopped talking. He wanted to go. The visit had depressed him.

Allington sat and played with a pencil, letting it roll across the table a little way in one direction and then back again.

He drew so beautifully, Stein thought. No one had prettier lines. So light and pure. It always looked like he was having fun drawing them.

Suddenly Allington asked, "How do you find the time?"

"Find the time? Well, it goes along all right. You develop a rhythm."

"I just thought," Allington said, "I just happened to think that, if you get stuck, I might be able to do a couple of strips. Sometime. If you'd like ..."

White Lady

They were probably about sixty years old and had clearly dressed for the evening. All three were exhilarated; the man driving the boat guessed they'd had a drink or two before leaving home. As he took them across, they talked a great deal and called him captain, and when they reached the dock they made a great to-do about going ashore and pretended to be afraid of falling in the water.

The restaurant lay on an islet in the middle of the harbour, an odd wooden pavilion with spire-topped towers and tall, extravagantly decorated windows. Now at dusk, the pale grey building was very pretty in a melancholy way. Ellinor said that it lay like a forgotten dream among its dark trees. Or maybe like a wedding cake on a plate that was too small. Ellinor loved similes.

"Yes, you're right!" May exclaimed. "That's just exactly what it looks like. A decorated cake. A gateau. Isn't that what we used to call them?"

"Good heavens, how pretty this is," Regina said. "Just look at the boats." They had walked onto the lawn, May,

Ellinor, and Regina, and were standing in a row on the wet grass. The harbour lights were soft and blurred in the evening fog, and against this backdrop of quivering lights, boats were gliding past, all of them on their way out to sea. Black coasting smacks and ketches, their sails like swans' wings, as Ellinor put it. And behind them came the overnight boat to Stockholm, tall, radiantly white, adorned with glowing strings of pearls. Slowly, slowly the great luxury liner glided out from the harbour with all the other boats around it, and every one of them had to swing wide to get past the islet where the three ladies stood. "Now let's go in," Regina said. "It's getting chilly."

The restaurant was empty; the season was almost over. They asked each other if they'd been here before, but only May remembered one time with her father, who'd been a member of the yacht club and had had his own boat berthed in the marina. The stairs were broad and the ceiling unbelievably high, almost like a church. Highest up, under the tower, was an intricate network of timbers. It was a warm evening, and the windows stood open along the entire length of the verandah. Fog drifted in across the empty tables.

"It's like some film I saw," Regina said. "A big castle with empty rooms and people who didn't know what they wanted."

"Marienbad," Ellinor said. "That was an awfully good movie. But why are you whispering?" They took seats at the far end of the verandah. The waiter came, and while they were ordering they found their way back to their initial exhilaration. They were going to eat and drink well, and for this one evening they had left everything behind and were going to enjoy themselves in a new, unusual place, an island from the turn of the century, a building that was almost old when they were children.

"That's what's so exciting," Regina said. "Having it all ahead of us. I'll have a White Lady. I'm wearing a white dress, so I want a White Lady."

"Is that strong?" May asked. "I'll have the same."

Regina called back the waiter to say she'd changed her mind – she wanted the pepper steak instead. And the wine should be at room temperature.

"Did you notice?" May said. "Did you notice how young the waiter was? In a place like this, they ought to be old. But he's young and quick and hears everything you say."

"I'm hungry," Ellinor said. "I'm always hungry. And I never have the nerve to order what I really want. I'm getting fat! And right now, after a real ocean voyage, I'm really especially hungry!" They all laughed, and then she said, suddenly sentimental, "The man driving the boat ... Just think! He'd been a captain on the seven seas. And then they let him go. He told me. Isn't that awful?"

May said, "You could use that in a book." She fished out her compact and quickly powdered her troubled little face, puffed up her hair, and put the purse on the floor beside her chair. "You're not a bit fat. You're sturdy."

"Junoesque," Regina said. "You know one time in Venice I drank a White Lady, or rather actually it was outside Venice in that casino, whatever it's called. That was my first White Lady. Cheers, girls! Anyway, there I was and I was so young they wouldn't let me in without an escort. Well, along came this bank director from Fiume ..."

"What?"

"Fiume. A bank director from Fiume. And I was young and sweet, so he invited me in and told me to bet as much as I wanted on roulette, because beginners always have such good luck, he said. It was foggy outside, just like this."

"Here comes the food!" May cried. "Girls, girls, this is going to be a real feast!"

The waiter smiled and asked which of them was to taste the wine.

"I'm the eldest," Ellinor said. "I'm several weeks older than any of you! I'm the Grand Old Lady." She sipped the wine and smiled at him and said, "Perfect. The temperature is just right. What shall we drink to?"

"To you!" Regina cried. "To your young people's books."

"How nice of you," Ellinor said. "Cheers. Though I don't know that anyone reads them any more. Have you noticed how the air smells of night?"

Regina said, "You have such beautiful thoughts. But it smells of the city. The sewers. It did in Venice, too, and it was just beautiful, beautiful ..."

May said they ought to change places. It was Ellinor who should sit opposite the window. The boats and all. "It could give you new ideas," May said. But Ellinor thought it was unnecessary. After a while they started talking about their friend the Count. It was some time since he'd called. "When was the last time he called you?"

"I don't know. Last spring. He's always so busy."

"Time," said Regina. "Speaking of time, that bank director from Fiume told me that the only thing he no longer had was time. He had everything else, money and everything, but he no longer had time. I didn't want to bet on roulette. I thought it was awful, so we went into the bar instead. 'Dear child,' he said. 'Pretty little child. Order whatever you'd like. Green, white, red, yellow.' That's exactly what he said. 'I have everything, but I also have a bad stomach.'"

"I know," said Ellinor.

"Do you also have a bad stomach?"

"No, but you've told that story before."

"Not to me," May said. "What did you order?"

"White. A White Lady. I thought it sounded so pretty. There was a little rim of ice on the glass. Look, there still is."

"About the Count," Ellinor said. "Has he called any of you?"

"Never," Regina said. "He's forgotten us. He's way too famous. We danced once. No, twice. Why don't they have any music here?"

Ellinor said, "They've been playing music the whole time – you just haven't heard it. Slow stuff on tape for the old folks. Ti-di-di-da, ti-di-di-da. Like in Marienbad."

"And foghorns," May said.

They listened. "Okay," Regina said, "it's foghorns. They're howling. How are they howling, Ellinor?"

"Like old, tired animals", Ellinor said, "that no longer have the strength to be afraid. Hey, what'll you give me for that one?"

"Ten plus!" May cried. "They're too tired even to be afraid. They just howl."

Regina stood up and said she was going to the ladies' room. On the way, she walked past the bar and asked if they didn't have any younger music. "So we won't feel so old," she added, and laughed. The waiter said that they had younger music but maybe it would make her feel even older. All the way downstairs, Regina wondered if he'd been cheeky, too familiar, and in that case, what she should have said. In any case it was too late now. The ladies' room was large and cool, tulle curtains knotted above the windows, each little stall provided with a faded family name, easy chairs covered in shiny chintz. Someone had left a red lifebelt hanging on a peg. Down here she cold hear the ships' foghorns much better. Regina grew melancholy. She stood and looked at her face in the neon light that made everything hard and hollow and thought it had been somehow less heavy in the old days. Her face had grown too long over the years, and her nose as well. She went back upstairs and said to the others, "I can't understand why he never calls."

"He's so rarely in town," Ellinor said. "But maybe we could dance."

"Speaking of dancing," Regina said. "That time. They couldn't stop playing to dance. There was an atmosphere of tension, a kind of fear, if you know what I mean.

The ones playing for high stakes, I mean insane sums of money, were fenced in with a rope. Four people with a fence around them so no one would disturb them. There was dead silence. No one dared say a word."

"How strange," May said. "Have you ever been back?"

"No. I thought about it once, but it never happened."

Some people came in at the other end of the verandah, very young people. "Like a flock of birds," said Ellinor, "a swarm of birds that settle for a moment, for as long as it suits them." The music suddenly changed to something entirely different. It had grown dark outside, and the harbour lights were sharp and distant. It was as if the island and the restaurant had slipped further out to sea, as if they were floating away.

"I'm so happy," May said. "It's as if nothing was important any more. Is this our second bottle?"

"Yes," Ellinor said.

The young people were not dancing. Why should they? They could afford not to. Wherever they went, their own music followed them. They talked quietly and were completely involved with one another.

"What would you say to an Irish coffee?" Regina said. "For the fun of it. You know, something unusual. I mean, now that the three of us are out together for once. She put her arms on the table and tried to sing along – ba-ding, ba-ding, doo-ah, doo-ah. "It's got a nice beat, doesn't it? Why don't they dance? The Count should be here."

"He's probably just polite," said Ellinor.

"Do you think any of them know you're an author? We could talk to them a little. *Garçon! Ciao.* Three Irish coffees. You don't get a lot of customers in the fall."

"No, not this late," the waiter said. "We'll be closing soon for the winter."

"Doesn't it get lonely here sometimes?" Regina said. "I mean, without customers. And all the rooms so large and nothing but empty chairs."

May said she'd imagined *whipped* cream. Some of the young people began to dance, almost absentmindedly, by themselves. Regina said she was going to the ladies' room.

"But you just came back."

She said, "I want to look around. It's not often I get to places like this." She walked over to the young people at the bar and said, "Hi, are you having a good time? Nice music, isn't it?"

"It's good," said a boy.

She took her White Lady with her, and as she passed their table she raised her glass and smiled, a little greeting, a disarming, dismissive gesture. "They're nice," she said when she came back. "Friendly and polite. We could treat them to something. I was always getting treated when I was young."

May said they hadn't whipped the cream, just stirred it in. It wasn't real Irish coffee. Now the music grew heavier, it forced itself upon them, stubbornly repeating the same phrases again and again, over and over. Ellinor said it was like a pulse.

"Then it's someone with a bad heart," May said. "He's not feeling well." She said she was going to the ladies' room to make herself pretty.

"Drink your Irish coffee while it's warm," Regina said. "And you're not going to get any prettier, neither here nor there."

"I don't want to drink it while it's warm. You're like my mother. I want to drink something clear and cold."

Regina said, "Green, white, red, yellow! Whatever you'd like." She laughed and threw herself back in her chair.

"Regina, you're drunk," Ellinor said.

Regina answered slowly. "I hadn't expected that. I really hadn't expected that from you. You're usually much more subtle."

"Girls, girls," May burst out. "Don't fight. Is anyone coming to the ladies with me?"

"Oh the ladies room, the eternal ladies' room," said Ellinor. "What do you do there all the time?" The whole scene was like something from an early talkie, with too much gesturing. It wasn't a very good film; the direction was definitely second-rate. "Just go," she said. "I want to look at the fog on the ceiling."

On their way to the stairs, Regina and May stopped at the bar. "Ciao," the waiter said, grinning. "What'll it be? Irish coffee?"

"Absolutely not," May said. She spoke with great care. "I would like a Cognac."

The tape stopped. Outside it was pitch-dark, a great autumn darkness. They stood with their backs to the bar. Regina raised her glass and cried, "Cheers for the springtime of youth! Cheers, everyone!"

They raised their glasses to her toast. One of them stood up and came to the bar. He looked at May and asked, "Are you the lady writer?" The waiter put on a new tape, an explosion of sound. Speech was out of the question; they smiled at each other. Ellinor appeared and shouted over the music, "What became of you? What are you doing here?"

Regina leaned towards the young man and shouted, "Here's the author! Ellinor! You all use first names these days, right? Another Cognac. One for you, too. Isn't this wonderful, just completely unreal? And you all dance so beautifully. This new way of dancing is so right. You just move, each person on his own. Like this ..."

The waiter laughed. The young man put down his glass and bowed to Regina.

"Here we go!" she called out playfully, in English.

They stood and looked for a while and then May said, "She's making a scene. Gyrating and carrying on. Ellinor, I don't feel well."

They went down to the ladies' room.

"Funny," Ellinor said. "I write books for young people and they don't know who I am. And I know nothing about them, either. Funny, isn't it?"

May had taken a seat in one of the chintz chairs. "What time is it?" she said. "But you don't write any more."

"I don't know. It's stopped."

"I admire you, but anyway ... Listen, I can't go in that motorboat. I don't feel well. It was the cream." After a while she said, "I detest Irish coffee. Have you got an aspirin?"

"No. They're in my other purse."

A young girl came in and went to the mirror. Ellinor asked if she had an aspirin.

"Terribly sorry," the girl said, "but I'm afraid I don't." She looked at May and said, "Is it her heart?"

May said, "Certainly not. There's nothing wrong with my heart. Anyway, I'm feeling better now." She went into one of the stalls and slammed the door behind her.

On the stairs she said, "Why should I have a problem with my heart? If someone wants an aspirin, it's because they've got a headache."

"Don't be angry," Ellinor said. "It was just the lighting."

Regina was sitting at the young people's table. She waved them over and called out, "Hi! Come here! Guess what, Peter's grandmother and my father knew each other! It's a small world, isn't it? This is Ellinor, who's a writer, and this is May." The young people stood and greeted them. One of them brought two extra chairs. "Now, let's go all in for gin!" Regina said, being playful in English again. "Ellinor? You're not in a bad mood, I hope. This is my friend Erik. He's just started at the university. What was it you were studying again?"

"Humanities."

"Oh yes. Humanities. The study of mankind. God, it's so lovely seeing nothing but pretty, friendly faces."

"You talk too much," Ellinor said.

The waiter turned up the music.

"Just look at these beautiful faces!" Regina cried. "I haven't seen such beautiful faces since I was in Venice!"

The young people got up to dance, as if on some common signal. The music was deafening, thudding, without melody. They danced solemnly. Unreachable, they moved with exquisite self-control.

"Like a ritual," Ellinor said.

"What did you say?" Regina yelled. "I can't hear you in this racket."

"A ritual!" Ellinor screamed. "Deadly serious. Priests and priestesses in the temple of Eros! Do you hear what I'm saying? I don't know a thing about books for young people and I want to pay the bill and go home!"

"What are you talking about?" May said. "Now I'm feeling ill again." But no one heard what she said. Regina shouted that she didn't want to go home. She had made a connection with the young people and wanted to share.

"Share what, for heaven's sake?" a weary Ellinor asked in Regina's ear, and Regina answered, "My experience! They listen to me!"

"I'm going to kill that waiter and his grin," said Ellinor. "Give us our bill. We're not friendly." He leaned over them, came so close it was hard to see what he looked like. "We can't stay," she said. "It's time for us to go."

"I'll pay for myself!" May shouted. "One for all and all for one ..."

They had turned out the lights in the main dining room and at the other end of the long verandah. Quick hands were stacking chairs, coming closer and closer, and now that it was dark it was even more apparent that the fog had entered the room.

"Dramatic," Ellinor said.

The bill came almost at once. When they stood up, the music abruptly stopped. The young people were standing on the dance floor looking at them. For several moments nothing happened and the silence was absolute.

"Thank you for a lovely evening," Regina said. "It's been wonderful." Suddenly she was shy. "A terribly important contact." She spoke slowly, with quiet dignity. "I'm certain that you've given my friend Ellinor many new ideas, and your charming thoughtfulness has made a deep impression on me, on us. And now we want to give you our best wishes for long lives and the best of everything."

The young man named Peter took several quick steps forward and kissed her hand. All the way down the stairs, the music was silent. Only when they were walking across the lawn did it come back in all its uncontrollable but now distant vitality.

Regina was crying. "Wasn't it wonderful?" she said. "Wasn't that simply wonderful? It was like in Venice. Do you know what he said to me? He'd taken me back to my hotel, a squalid little place, but I thought it was splendid, and his stomach was hurting him the whole time, and then he said, 'Dear, sweet girl, if I'd been thirty years younger, our evening would have ended in a different way.' Wasn't that too bad? You understand, he was really having trouble with his stomach. And the next morning he sent roses, dozens of roses, the first flowers anyone ever sent me."

"I understand," Ellinor said. "But now you need to pull yourself together. The boat's coming."

"Look!" May cried. "There it comes. Isn't it like Charon's ferry or something? You like similes."

"By all means," Ellinor said. She was tired and in no mood for anyone's similes but her own.

The Doll's House

ALEXANDER WAS AN UPHOLSTERER of the old school. He was exceptionally skilled, and he took a craftsman's natural pride in his work. He discussed commissions only with those customers who had taste and a feel for the beauty of materials and workmanship. Not wishing to show his contempt, he referred all the others to his employees.

His workshop was old. It lay in a cellar, down a flight of stairs from the pavement, but it was quite large. He was never short of work. Alexander himself took responsibility for ornamentation in wood and for difficult upholstering. Simpler jobs he assigned to others. There were still some people who wanted hand-crafted decoration – there weren't many, but they existed. They could be very particular about, say, the choice of wallpapers. Alexander gave them time. He conducted long, detailed discussions about the right background for period furniture. Occasionally he left the shop to attend auctions or to browse the best antique shops, and wherever he went, whether to buy or, with his silence, to reject, he was an honoured guest. The most beautiful pieces found their way to his apartment, a place very few people had visited. It lay on a quiet street in the southern part of the city. For twenty years, Alexander had shared the apartment with his friend Erik, and both men had the same respect for the lovely objects that time and Alexander's insight had gathered around them.

Sometimes Alexander would sit and read while at work. He read the classics, the French and the German among others, but primarily the Russian, which enchanted him with their heavy patience. They gave him a sense of the ineluctable constancy of things. With his thick eyebrows furrowed and his short, powerful body expressing concentration and voluntary solitude, he read during working hours and no one dared disturb him.

When Alexander retired, he sold his workshop judiciously and after mature reflection. He took with him quite a number of product samples of various kinds – old-fashioned tassels and braiding, books of wallpapers and ornamentation. Most of it was quite dated, but it had a beauty few people could see. At about the same time, Erik retired from the bank. They put Alexander's samples in a cupboard and drank champagne to celebrate their new freedom.

It was difficult in the beginning. They weren't used to spending their days together with nothing to do, and it all felt wrong. Erik's eyes ached from watching television, and Alexander was most interested in Russian films. They bought a stereo and listened their way gropingly through piles of cassettes and LPs that they had purchased quite possibly because of an attractive jacket. Their friends Jani and Pekka gave them tips, and they admired the music but didn't like it, at least not enough that they longed to hear it.

"Turn it off," Alexander said. "I can't read." But in fact he didn't care about reading as much as he once had. Perhaps books had tantalized him only as a stolen luxury in the middle of a working day.

"You're not turning the pages," Erik said. "Are you unhappy about something?" His voice was always the same – low, gentle, thoughtful. His strong eyeglasses reflected the light and hid the expression in his eyes.

"No," Alexander said. "I'm not unhappy. Leave it on if you want."

"No," Erik said. "I don't think I do."

Erik did the cleaning. He polished the furniture, and every morning he ran his vacuum over the rugs. The mornings were best. They threw open all the windows, and, while they drank their morning coffee and shared the newspaper, Erik planned lunch and dinner, sometimes asking Alexander for advice. Alexander would laugh and say, "You decide. Surprise me. I've never been disappointed." Erik went to the shop on the corner or to the covered market, which was further away. Sometimes they'd have Jani and Pekka for supper and play the stereo. But there were always the long days.

It was sometime in September that Alexander began work on the doll's house. That is to say, he didn't know it would become a doll's house. He made a little oval table in mahogany with a carved base and then two Victorian chairs that he covered in red velvet.

Erik said, "They're tiny and yet completely accurate. I don't understand how you do it. But we don't know any children."

"What do you mean?" Alexander said.

"I mean, what are you going to do with them?"

"I just made them," Alexander replied. "How about some coffee?"

He made a cabinet with glass doors. He made an étagère with hand-carved knobs. The parlour table where he worked was covered with newspapers, and Erik vacuumed the rugs twice a day. Finally they agreed that Alexander would move his toys out to the kitchen. Every morning after coffee in the parlour, he went straight out to the kitchen and went to work. He made an upholstered sofa and a little bed of thin brass tubing with round knobs. There was a moment when he thought he'd let Erik make the mattress, but mattresses are precise and difficult things. Erik was all thumbs when it came to anything other than numbers and housekeeping. So Alexander said nothing and made the mattress himself.

He made more and more furniture, more and more exquisite parlour furniture, kitchen furniture, verandah furniture, and, finally, old-fashioned furniture to store in the attic or hide away on a staircase. Alexander constructed all of it with the same loving care and attention. He made windows. French windows, attic windows, Carelian gingerbread windows, stupid ordinary windows

– every sort. And doors. Complex or very simple doors, Wild-West doors, and classic Greek portals.

Erik said, "I understand the furniture, but why are you making doors and windows? They don't lead anywhere. And why can't you clean up after yourself when you're done?"

"That's an idea," Alexander said. "I've got an idea." And he left everything where it was and went into the parlour and turned on the stereo. "This is lovely music," he said, but he wasn't listening.

"Turn it off!" Erik cried, and Alexander turned it off and went on thinking. He was imagining a house, the ultimate house. But he'd make no blueprints. The house would be allowed to grow however it wished, organically, room by room. The natural thing would be to start with the cellar. Alexander gathered materials. He went out to an abandoned stonemasonry at the edge of town and collected pretty shards of stone for the foundation. He assembled lumber – aspen, balsa, and pine – and he filled the kitchen cabinets with bottles and jars containing various glues, paints, and solvents. He was more and more in the way. Erik said the kitchen was not a hobby room, it was impossible to run the house without space to work in, and he didn't want sawdust in the food. They agreed to divide the kitchen in two with a partition that reached almost to the ceiling. The window was on Erik's side, but Alexander bought some powerful lighting. He also managed to manoeuvre a workbench into his cubicle. The kitchen cabinet on his side had to be emptied, and all its china was piled on improvised shelves in the kitchen.

Alexander spent a long time arranging his tools lovingly in the cabinet, each tool easy to reach in its own appropriate place. He built the cellar and began on a miniature woodworking shop. In the middle of the wall dividing their kitchen, Alexander had built a little window, and from time to time he would look out and say, "Hi, what's for lunch?" Or Erik would look in and say, "What are you making now?" And Alexander would carefully place the world's smallest finishing plane in Erik's hand to be admired and remarked upon.

When finished, the miniature woodshop was very small, with a sloping roof. Alexander had built it with bleached wood and taken great pains to give it a window with dirty panes that were broken in just the right way. It had a tree stump for chopping wood and a workbench with tiny tools, each of them exact to the tiniest detail. He had never before felt such peace of mind. He liked the quiet. Sometimes the telephone would ring out in the apartment, as if in another world.

"That was Jani and Pekka on the phone. We should have them to dinner sometime soon."

"Yes, of course," Alexander answered. "As soon as I've finished the woodshop." He sat up half of every night, having fun, never turning on the television. He ate too fast and went back to his cubby as quickly as he could. Erik bought new cassettes and turned up the volume louder and louder. When Alexander came into the bedroom at night, he was preoccupied and happy and fell asleep at once. Early in the morning, he was back at work. He took his coffee through the window.

"But where are you?" Erik said. He pushed a cup of coffee and some sandwiches across the windowsill. Alexander caught a glimpse of his troubled face and long nose, but his glasses turned his eyes to empty mirrors.

"What did you say?" he asked.

"Where are you? Where are you these days?"

"On the second floor," Alexander said. "I'm up in the kitchen. The trapdoor in the floor is really a challenge. It has to meet the cellar stairs."

"Of course," said Erik.

"What do you mean, 'of course'? In that tone of voice."

Erik was silent. Then he said, "It was nothing. What does it look like, the trapdoor?"

Alexander showed him. The trapdoor was laid in the kitchen floor with miniature hinges, while a thin chain prevented it from falling open. The stairway down to the cellar, meticulously mounted, disappeared in darkness.

"It's lovely," Erik said. "Where did you get this doll's house idea?"

"It's not a doll's house," Alexander said immediately. "It's a house."

"Who for?"

"Just a house. Maybe for us. I'm building everything exactly the way I want it. I decide. The first and second storeys are by the sea. Then comes the parlour."

"Where?"

Alexander laughed a little. "Somewhere in Germany. The attic will be in Paris. We'll see."

Erik looked into the kitchen. "It has a wood stove."

"Of course. It's prettier."

"Good lord," Erik said. "I can't imagine cooking on a wood stove. It's impossible. Not when you're used to a modern kitchen."

"You'll get used to it," Alexander said.

He never swept his workshop. Wood curls and sawdust and stone dust lay like a thick fur rug on the floor, and he liked standing in this soft soil his work had created and letting it grow thicker and deeper around him. He trailed it over the rest of the apartment and Erik had to vacuum several times a day.

When the kitchen ceiling was finished, Alexander began thinking about electric lights. The house should definitely have electricity. He bought materials, thin copper wire, fixtures, and flashlight batteries, and spent a lot of time wiring the first and second storeys. It was not a success. He had to remove the wiring in the kitchen ceiling, and he damaged the stairs in the process. Erik thought the house could be lit just as well from the outside.

"Out of the question," Alexander said. "This house has to glow, it has to live from the inside, don't you see? We're there inside, and other people walk by outside. But these batteries aren't worth a damn. Or else there's something wrong with the wiring."

In the end he called Jani. Jani had an electrician friend called Boy. Boy came and had a look. "You've got to get rid of all this junk," he said. "It's never going to work. You're going to need a transformer on the bottom floor." He explained in detail. They were absorbed in their electrical discussions all evening and went on planning during supper.

"This will be a piece of cake," Boy said. "You haven't got a clue, but I'll teach you. I'll get it working. But you're going to have to take up that middle floor again because of the wiring. You're a wonderful carpenter, but you don't know a damn thing about electricity."

Boy came back almost every evening. He often brought little table lamps, sconces, or a chandelier that he'd found in some hobby shop or toy store. He came straight from work in his jeans and trailed street dirt over the rugs, but Alexander didn't seem to notice – he just admired whatever Boy had brought with him and listened gravely to his suggestions about improvements to the house.

"You should realize", Boy said, "that this house is going to be famous. But whatever you build, it's the lighting that's going to make it sing. Believe me."

Boy was a little, skinny fellow. He looked and moved a bit like a squirrel. He laughed often, showing his gums all the way to the roof of his mouth, and he clapped them both chummily on the back. Erik detested being clapped on the back, especially by such a small man wearing boots with high heels. When Boy came, the three of them would sit in the parlour and talk for a while, about whatever, about nothing, the way people do when they're ready to leave but want to round things off to be polite. And then Alexander would stand up and say maybe they should get started and he'd go into his little cubbyhole with Boy. The tone of their voices changed, grew quieter and calmer, and the pauses grew longer. They stood and thought, considering some problematic detail in their construction project.

From electrical, they had moved on to concern themselves with the uprights in a bay window and the construction of a spiral staircase. Out in the kitchen, Erik was preparing supper. The window to the cubby was closed on account of the sawdust, so he could only hear their voices, not what they were saying. But in their exchange of practical questions and suggestions, he could hear a quiet and complete harmony of purpose. Often these unheard, intermittent conversations were like breezes passing through foliage – strengthening, fading, stopping, then quickening again. From time to time, Boy would laugh, the way a person laughs when something finally fits.

By December, Alexander had reached the parlour. He made French windows and put different colours of cellophane in the complex pattern of panes. Erik went into the cubicle and said, "About the cellar. I was cleaning the medicine cabinet and found some little bottles that are empty. We could put jam in them. You know, something we could colour red. And then cover them with paper and put on labels."

"Excellent!" Alexander exclaimed. "Great idea! You can use plaster. I'll show you how to mix it."

Erik set to work on his jam jars on the kitchen counter. He did a fine job, and each time he finished a jar and had written a label, he would take it to the window and get it approved. Finally Alexander said that now they had enough jam jars, and when they went on coming he was irritated. "We're in the middle of a really difficult bit right now," he said. "We don't have time for jam jars. Can't you find something else to do?"

Erik walked straight out of the kitchen and turned on the television in the parlour. It was a lecture about the metal industry. After a while, Alexander came after him and said that the cellar needed some apples. But not too many. They could probably be made from clay, but don't make the clay too wet and hard to handle. Erik's apples weren't great, and neither were his cucumbers, bananas and melons. But when they'd been painted and piled out of the way behind the cellar stairs, it didn't much matter.

The house rose higher and higher. It had reached the attic, now, and had grown more and more fantastic. Alexander was in love, almost obsessed, with the thing he was trying to create. When he woke up in the morning, his first thought was The House, and he was instantly occupied with the solution to some problem of framing or a difficult staircase or the spire on a tower. Never before had he felt so light and free. Even his night thoughts, in the past often burdened with anxiety or self-reproach, had changed. He had only to close his eyes and walk into his house and see that everything was as it should be. In his imagination, critical faculties sharpened to their limit, he would walk attentively from room to room, up stairways, out onto balconies; he would examine every detail and see that each was completed and that the whole was astonishingly beautiful. He saw the tower that would ultimately rise above his work and crown it triumphantly. Sometimes at night he would get up, very quietly so as not to wake Erik, and sneak into the kitchen, into his cubby. He would turn on a flashlight, sit on a kitchen chair, and look. He'd shine the flashlight through one window after another as if it were moonshine or the beam of a lighthouse. Alexander was in the grip of a passion for perfection. He was not aware of how closely, how perilously, perfectionism and fanaticism are related.

Erik was allowed to sand window frames and paint them white. Once he tried to hang wallpaper on a landing, but it wrinkled and had to be pulled off.

When the elaborate attic storey began taking shape, The House was nearly two metres tall and would no longer fit in Alexander's cubby. Alexander and Boy had a long talk and decided the only alternative was to empty the bedroom.

"It'll fit exactly," Alexander said. "We can put the workbench under the window. And it won't fit in the parlour."

"Which parlour?" Erik said. "Yours or mine?"

"What's your problem?" Alexander said. "What are you angry about? This is important. We're about to start on the tower." He borrowed two collapsible camp beds and put them in the hall. They lifted the big double bed in the bedroom and leaned it against the wall. The House was moved with infinite care and placed on a modelling stand with a revolving top. Now, in full daylight, The House changed character. The dreamlike quality was replaced by a bewildering impression of lifelikeness. The flat winter light filled every room. The pillars and the long balustrade on the open gallery threw pale grey shadows that were real, and the green, red and blue panes in the windows cast soft rainbows on the floor. Every detail, every article of furniture, became convincing, as if they had all stood in place for generations. Alexander rotated The House slowly on its platform.

"And now," he said, "now we've come to the attic. Now we build our tower."

Boy said, "The cupola won't be easy. It'll have to be asymmetrical. Otherwise we won't have room for the tower and the new gallery."

"True," said Alexander. "We've got our work cut out for us. Which room do you think we should make smaller?"

"The bedroom. We'll have to make it a lot smaller."

"That's wrong!" Erik said. "Completely wrong. I don't agree at all. The bedroom's already too small, and the window's too high!"

"About the cupola," Alexander went on. "You may be right that we could make it asymmetrical."

"Yes," Boy said. "I mean, so we'll have room for our gallery." And they bent over the workbench and started sketching the tricky section of the roof.

That evening, Erik had not prepared any supper. He said he had a headache. They could make something themselves or eat something cold from the pantry.

"Did you take an aspirin?" Alexander asked.

"Yes, of course," Erik said. He was lying on the sofa in the parlour, staring at the ceiling with his feet on the armrest. And he hadn't taken off his shoes. Alexander went for a blanket. "Lift your feet," he said, and he put a newspaper over the arm of the sofa.

The next day, Alexander suggested that Erik sew curtains for The House, even though he knew that Erik had never sewn and couldn't even hem a tablecloth.

The winter wore on and The House rose higher and higher. Alexander and Boy had moved beyond the cupola and were working on the highest tower, where they were planning a rotating beacon. Their Black & Deckers ran every evening, an infernal shrieking of electric saws and drills in the bedroom, interrupted by periodic silence. Erik sat and watched television. Sometimes he went to the local cinema. Alexander asked if he couldn't go and visit Jani and Pekka or some of their other friends, but Erik didn't want to. "Anyway," he said, "it's our turn to invite them."

"Yes, yes, I know," said Alexander, "but not until The House is finished. Then they can come and look. I've told you, we can't be disturbed while we're building."

Boy didn't seem to notice that anything was wrong. He was cheerful and chatty at mealtimes and completely occupied with getting the beacon to rotate.

One evening when Alexander had gone to the station to buy cigarettes, Boy threw open the door to the parlour and shouted, "It's going around! It's rotating! We've done it!"

Erik turned off the television. In the darkened room he walked slowly towards Boy and then past him into the bedroom, where the only lights were in The House, lamps burning on every floor. From the final, topmost tower, red and green lights swept across the walls of the bedroom in a steady rhythm.

"We did it!" Boy shouted, laughing out loud. "Alexander and me! We made it work. We've topped off the house and the beacon's working just the way it should. Well? What do you think of our house?"

"It's not yours," said Erik very softly.

"Oh yes it is," Boy said. "It sure is! You'd better believe it is! Come and look from the other side. Come look at the way the lights reflect in the bedroom mirrors!" When Erik didn't move, he took him by the arm.

"Don't touch me!" Erik shouted.

"Don't be silly," Boy said, and gave him a slap on the back. Erik screamed – a little, squeaky scream. Fumbling on the workbench he grabbed a tool, something that felt hard and cold in his hand, and he flew at Boy and struck at him blindly. The drill bit hit him near the ear and angled down towards his shoulder, and Boy threw himself back against the doll's house, which tottered for a moment and seesawed on its podium. The beacon continued to rotate. Boy jumped behind the doll's house and yelled, "Stop that, for Christ's sake! Have you lost your mind?"

Erik pursued him step by step. It was hard for him to see, and the moving beacon distorted the room and made it seem strange. He stumbled. Boy was silent.

"I know where you are," Erik said. "You're hiding behind the doll's house." He gripped the drill shaft harder and went after him. "I'm coming," he said. "And this time I won't miss."

"Jesus Christ! Leave me alone," Boy said. He was trapped in a corner of the room and couldn't get away. "What do you want?"

Erik began to tremble. All he knew was that he had to strike out, just once, one time, but hard. There was something wrong with his glasses, all he could see was the beacon fluttering round and round. "Turn off that damned light," he screamed.

Boy didn't move.

"Turn it off so I can see you, or I'll smash the whole tower to pieces!" He took one step towards Boy and said, "Shall I smash you or the tower?" By now he was shaking so hard he could barely stand. "Shall I smash you to pieces? Is it you I should smash?"

"No," Boy said. "Not me."

Erik took off his glasses. They were in the way – they'd fogged up and made it hard to see. The everyday act of taking off his glasses and stuffing them in his pocket altered everything, inexplicably. A great weariness swept over him, and he said, "Could you go turn on the overhead light? There's something wrong with my glasses."

When the light came on, he put the drill handle back on the workbench. Boy put his fingers carefully to his ear and looked at his hand. "Blood," he said. "It's running down on my collar."

Erik sat down on the floor. He felt ill.

They heard the front door open. A few moments later, Alexander came in, stopped in the doorway and said, "What the hell's going on in here?"

"He hit me," Boy said. "Look! Blood!"

"Erik?" said Alexander. "Why are sitting on the floor? Where are your glasses?"

"In my pocket. I feel sick."

"What have you done?"

"I don't know," Erik said. "But I saved our tower. It's all in one piece."

Slowly, Alexander opened a pack of cigarettes, took one out and lit it. "It actually rotates," he said. "You know your stuff, Boy. Now the whole thing's perfect. No one's ever built such a house as Erik's and mine."

A Sense of Time

FIRST AND FOREMOST, you need to understand that I really love my grandmother. I love her honestly and respectfully, and for the most part I understand the things about her that are hard to understand. We've lived together all my conscious life. But I have no idea what it is that has so completely upset her sense of time, and I'm sure she hasn't, either. We never talk about it.

How should I begin so you won't misunderstand ...? First of all, you mustn't think any of this is funny! Before I say too much, there's one thing I want you to remember. Grandmother is the calmest and happiest person you can imagine. Sometimes I think it is precisely this – that she's lost her grip on time, I mean – that keeps her happy.

Since my parents died, Grandmother has taken care of me in the sweetest way. We've lived together for seventeen years, and she is now very old. In the beginning, I took it all in my stride. If she woke me in the middle of the night and wanted to take a mid-morning stroll, I followed along without a question. I got used to it – in fact, I loved our nocturnal rambles. I was proud of being the only child out at night. Mostly we went to the park or down to the harbour; Grandmother knew I was interested in boats. I remember her high-topped shoes on the pavement. As we walked down the street, they made the only sound. The streets were always empty except for an occasional passing car. I also grew accustomed to her serving me my evening tea in the middle of the day and then putting me to bed and drawing the curtains. I would read under the covers with a flashlight. Then it got worse. I realized that Grandmother had completely lost her sense of time, and I began to object. That distressed and upset her. Indeed it confused her, and I couldn't stand to see her anxious, so after that I let her divide up the day whatever way she liked.

When I entered the university – that was a year ago – she interfered with my work a great deal. I would get up at six o'clock, sit down to study, and she would come in and worry that I was staying up too late. "You need to go to bed," she'd say. "You need to rest your eyes and your poor nerves. There's no hurry, you've plenty of time to study, believe me. Can't you please go to bed if Grandmother asks you very nicely?"

This doesn't happen every day, but still several times a week. Grandmother's private, interior world must be very strong if she can so serenely deny the sun and the moon. I wonder what it is that shines for her and makes her so terribly certain and calm. I don't want to upset her, far from it, but lately it's become a real nuisance. I try to organize my work day according to a schedule, a kind of supporting framework of sometimes rather fragile decisions built on good intentions and exertion. It all falls apart when Grandmother wakes me at night and gives me a cup of coffee to make it easier for me to get up. It destroys my concentration. I'm sure you know what I mean.

Today I am really upset. Grandmother and I have a long flight ahead of us, all the way to Anchorage, Alaska. She wants to see an old friend who is very dear to her. He's a doctor, although he's now an old man and gave up his practice long ago. Grandmother is generally frightened of doctors, but she believes in this man. He saved her life once, when she had diphtheria. She says they could always talk to each other in a clear and secret way that no one else could understand. Now I'm hoping that he'll be able to help us. He has taken care of people who are not exactly out of their minds, but not exactly in their minds, either, if you know what I mean. People with misconceptions or, let us say, dislocations in the ability to perceive and make judgements – in other words, the sort of thing that can affect otherwise completely social, well-meaning individuals. Of course, Grandmother is not going to see him as a patient. She just wants to visit him before she's too old to travel.

It was hard getting Grandmother to the plane. She insisted it was a night flight, that she'd always wanted to see the North Pole at night, that we were leaving way too early and would have to wait at the airport for hours. I tried to explain. I showed her the timetable and a world map. Nothing helped. Finally I pleaded with her to come for my sake, and then she came. Our plane was delayed, or maybe it was being repaired. Grandmother fell asleep wrapped in a blanket, but every time they'd call out an arrival or departure over their ghastly loudspeakers, she would jump to her feet anxiously and look at me until I calmed her down and explained that we still had plenty of time.

Now she's sitting in the window seat on the aeroplane and I've bundled her up well. Every time she wakes up, she can see the North Pole. A little while ago, the stewardess handed out pretty cards guaranteeing that the passenger has really flown right over the pole – two polar bears in relief stare up at a vanishing aeroplane, white on white in a compass-like frame. I'm saving the card for her. When I was little, we collected pretty postcards and pinned them to a bulletin board. Many of them came from Grandmother's friend in Alaska. He travelled a lot when he was young. I remember in particular a beach in Hawaii and the Place de la Concorde after dark.

It is now deep night. There is a full moon sharply outlined against a black sky, and, 36,000 feet below us, the snow. Hour after hour, the same empty bluish white expanse. They've turned off the overhead lights, and now one can see that the snow down there is not a completely smooth surface. Sometimes the moonlight throws long shadows.

Before we left, Grandmother talked a lot about the arctic night we would fly through. "Isn't it a mystical word, 'arctic'? Pure and quite hard. And meridians. Isn't that pretty? We're going to fly along them, faster than the light can follow us. Isn't that right? Time won't be able to catch us." She is enjoying the trip immensely. This is, in fact, the first time she's ever flown. The most interesting part to her was the meal, which was served on a tray with depressions like soap dishes for each item. She put the minimal salt and pepper shakers in her purse, also the little plastic spoons. "They're spoiling us," she said. "They're always giving us something – a candy, a newspaper, a glass of juice ..."

Of course, I've noticed that the stewardess gives us much more attention than she gives the other passengers, probably because Grandmother is so old – in an open, almost charming way – and because she's so delighted with everything they give her.

Grandmother's friend is going to meet us in Anchorage, then we change planes and the three of us fly on to Nome, where he lives. I'm very tense. Is she going to talk to him about time, perilous time? Does she realize how dangerous she's made it? Is she hoping he'll straighten the whole thing out or, to the contrary, tell her she's right? Dear heaven, I hope he doesn't upset her.

I think I'll sleep a little. I'm so terribly tired. Almost everyone is sleeping; the whole plane is quiet.

My watch has stopped.

♦♦♦

Grandmother woke up. Beneath her stretched an endless landscape of snow. The sky just above the horizon was brown with a dark red kernel that cut through the night right under the wing in the direction the plane was flying. The stewardess walked by, stopped, and smiled at Grandmother. Grandmother smiled back and with a finger to her lips indicated that her grandson needed his sleep; he was very tired. The stewardess nodded and walked on. The long blue field of snow was intensely cold against its glowing horizon. It was like a landscape in a dream, one of those endless dreams where everything stands and waits. Grandmother let her thoughts move on to John, wondering in what way he'd grown old. But she was sure she'd know him again at once.

By and by, the ice field below was interrupted by belts of dark water, and the sea opened up more and more. Grandmother sat whispering to herself. "Lonely schooners of ice and snow ..." she whispered. "To see the coast of Alaska ... Night in Nome."

The plane lurched and seemed to fall, then rose again and flew on with its wings bouncing up and down as if in the grip of some powerful, capricious storm. Lennart woke up. "Don't be afraid, it's nothing to worry about!" he said. "It has something to do with warm and cold air as we come in over the coast."

"Temperature changes," said Grandmother. "I understand."

Lennart leaned across and looked down at the alien landscape. Mountains now, white and conical, beautifully drawn, one behind the other, as simple as a child's drawing, the red horizon glowing behind them.

"The sun's coming up," he said.

"No, darling," Grandmother said, "it's going down. That's what's so interesting. We're coming out of a long arctic night, and when we catch up with the day it's already evening."

Lennart looked at his grandmother and, unable to control his frustration, he burst out, "Why aren't you wearing your seatbelt? Why don't you ever do what I say? You don't listen!" He fastened her belt and started gathering up their magazines, stood up and rummaged through the luggage bin for gloves and hats. Finally he tried to put on his overcoat, but lost his balance and sat down abruptly as the plane banked. It was unbearably warm and he felt a little ill.

"This turbulence won't last long," the stewardess said. "But you must keep your safety belts fastened."

"Lennart," said Grandmother, "the next time we fly, do you think they'd let us into the cockpit just for a little while? And when we land, do you think you could find some nice postcards of the sunset?"

"Yes, yes," Lennart said. "Whatever you want. I'll take care of it. I'll fix it." He was wet with sweat halfway down his back.

They landed in Anchorage.

Grandmother was unsteady on her legs because she'd been sitting still too long. He was trying to hold her arm, and at the same time carry all their bags and belongings. The stream of people was steered into a narrow corridor, a kind of tunnel that led into the arrivals hall. He couldn't find their tickets at the check point – there was a long delay, and when he finally found them and they moved on he couldn't see the departure time for the next flight because he couldn't find his glasses. He should have checked earlier. He ought to find someone who could get Grandmother a chair. There didn't seem to be a single chair in the whole hall, only glass walls and doors everywhere, and people pushing forward in the queue and kicking their bags along over the slippery floor and into the backs of a person's knees, suddenly impatient as if seconds mattered. It was unforgivable that he hadn't checked and remembered when the connecting flight was to leave for Nome. The loudspeakers bellowed constantly. People were divided up into queues marked "Transit" or "Exit" or were crowded together into a waiting room. He held onto Grandmother and they were channeled into a large echoing space decorated with skins and icicles. And there stood John, waiting for them, a little old man with a white goatee. John saw them at once and walked up to Grandmother and kissed her hand. They sat down at a table and looked at each other.

"Grandmother," said Lennart, "I'll be right back. I'm just going to buy our postcards." In the corridor he found no one selling cards, mostly just hides and little stuffed polar bears and seals. He hurried on through the transit hall, where people sat eating, and up a flight of stairs. He should have found his glasses and checked departure times. The stairs went down again and he walked through swinging doors and found himself in a new hall with nothing but panelling and posters on the walls. The high panels looked like doors, but they didn't give when he pushed on them and they had no handles. He ran around the room a couple of times before he saw the blue lamp over the exit, which led him straight out into the snow. There were several trucks beside a snow bank. It could have been a loading area. In any case no lights, just black night. An aeroplane rose towards the sky behind the terminal. The red horizon had faded and there was nothing but deep arctic night. He turned and ran back – up the stairs and down a corridor and into a new hall that he didn't recognize. Now it was just a question of finding Grandmother and getting her onto the flight to Nome and finding out when it left. They needed to hurry, and Grandmother moved slowly and got ill if you tried to rush her. He tried not to listen to the arrival and departure announcements. He kept repeating Grandmother's lovely, magically effective words – *arctic, mystical meridians, Nome at night.* He kept running and finally found his way back and saw them sitting side by side, Grandmother and John. They were deep in conversation. He walked up to them and stood behind Grandmother's chair and heard her say, "They're equally lovely. Day and night are equally beautiful to me. But Lennart needs to learn where they belong. You understand, he's only just begun to live his life in earnest, and it will be so awkward for him if he doesn't get help ..."

"Grandmother," Lennart said, "there weren't any cards."

"Don't worry," she said. "John has cards for us."

They lay there on the table, the sun shining across the ice. A red sun touching the horizon, its mirror image in the blue ice.

"We should go now," John said. "But there's no hurry. We've plenty of time."

A Leading Role

IT WAS THE BIGGEST PART she'd ever been given, but it didn't suit her, it didn't speak to her. An insignificant, anxious, middle-aged woman, an obliterated creature without any personality whatsoever! She had one good scene in the third act, but the rest of it! A shadow – to play a shadow in her first leading role. She called Sanderson and said, "It's Maria. I've read through the part and I think it's lifeless. Maybe it's literature, but it's not theatre."

"I knew you'd say that," Sanderson replied. "I've been waiting for you to call. Now listen to me. This is your big chance, and you're going to take it. And it *is* theatre, great theatre."

"Oh, really," she said. "I'm so glad you told me. It's one of his short stories that he's rehashed into a play. But he can't write for the stage."

"You're going to have to let us decide that," Sanderson said. He was determined to take no nonsense from Maria. She was professional and she could take direction, but there wasn't a whole lot more to her than that, which she ought to understand herself. He said, "You can count on the director. Go through the play again and call me. We need to make a decision this week to get the autumn season set."

Two days later, Maria Mickelson called and accepted the part.

It was early summer, and she had driven out to their country house to open it for the season. The weather was dreadful, an ice-cold fog as grey and impenetrable as the role of Ellen. Down by the dock, the reeds vanished out into the empty nothingness of the lake, and the spruce trees were black with moisture. The fog forced its way into the house, and the fire wouldn't burn. She let it all go, poured herself a drink and sat down on the sofa with her coat around her shoulders. The whole house was a mistake. It was too big, it had never been modernized, and it was too far from town. But Hans was fond of it – childhood home, and all that. Fishing on the weekends, dinner and sauna with his friends from the office. Jovial chatter with the local boatmen and fishermen. So how was your winter? Getting any whitefish in your nets? Doesn't that look like a storm off to the southwest?

She had spoken to him. "Don't you see how isolated we're going to be? I'm not interested in fishing, or gardening either. And there aren't any neighbours to socialize with." And he said, "Why not invite someone you like to come and stay? Someone from the theatre? One of your relatives? You know such an awful lot of people." It was true. But she didn't much care for them. They were all right in the city, but not at close quarters in a summer house. She had tried. And every time it was a relief when they finally left. Relatives were out of the question – childish, middle-class mediocrities who admired her, vaguely, without a clue about her actual work. It must be wonderful to be an actress! What an exciting life! I could just *never* appear on stage! Learning all those lines by heart!...Only her cousin Frida was quiet. Quiet and adoring. A grey little mouse with frightened eyes.

Maria pulled her coat tighter about her shoulders and raised her glass. And at that moment it came to her, a perfectly simple, straightforward insight. She put her glass down again and sat quite still. Cousin Frida. Cousin Frida was the consummate model for the role of Ellen. She *was* Ellen. Her gestures, her walk, the way she held her head, her voice, all of it! Maria Mickelson laughed out loud, finished her drink, and stood up. She walked to the mirror and studied herself, her well-groomed regular features, and the first, fine network of lines that middle age had drawn about her eyes and mouth. A new hairdo, grey-brown and badly cut, like Frida's ... shoulders drawn up, nervous hands ... How was it Frida moved her hands, that furtive, automatic gesture towards her mouth? And her way of holding a glass? Sitting down in a chair?

How would this sound? Dear cousin Frida, it's altogether too long since we last spoke. My dear, we mustn't just let time go by and lose touch. But now I've had a wonderful idea that I hope you'll agree to. Couldn't you take some time off work and come out here for a week or so? Everything's starting to bloom, and it will be warm soon ...

◆◆◆

But the warm weather didn't come. The fog lay just as tight around the house when Frida arrived. Maria paid close attention to her cautious way of stepping off the bus, her exaggerated gratitude when the driver helped her with her bag. Her clothes were right, in fact perfect. Not too unpretentious. There was an actual attempt at a modest elegance – a misguided attempt.

I'll skip the glasses, she thought, that would be overkill. But I can keep the way she peeks over them. I can use that.

"Welcome," she said. "It's been much too long. Let me take your suitcase. It's not far ..."

"No, by no means," Frida exclaimed. "What an idea!" She was obviously nervous. "It was so nice of you to invite me," she said. "You have so many friends."

The spruce forest was very dark, the trees closing them in on every side.

I need to write down my observations. Even the tiniest ones; they're the most important. Every day.

She said, "Let's see how you like your room. It looks out on the lake. It's still a bit chilly, but I've laid a fire."

"How kind," Frida said. "But you really mustn't go to any trouble, I don't usually mind the cold ... I mean, generally ..." An unfinished sentence, voice trailing off to silence.

"It'll be fine," Maria said. "I'm so truly pleased you could come."

◆◆◆

The house was white with a black roof, tall and rather narrow, with steep stairs leading up to a long verandah. In bad weather, pressed against a wall of spruce, it was a gloomy house. In front of the verandah, the ground sloped down towards the dock and the water.

"Is that really the ocean?" cousin Frida asked shyly, squinting into the fog. "I've never stayed right beside the real ocean."

"The open water's further out," Maria explained. "But our bay is quite large. The boat's being repaired. As soon as it warms up a bit, Hans will bring it out."

"But, now in the fog, it's almost like the open ocean anyway," her cousin said and smiled. Her smile radiated a great, relaxed friendliness and altered her entire face. She turned around and contemplated the house, holding her suitcase in front of her with both hands.

"The house doesn't look its best at the moment," Maria said, suddenly irritated. "It's really made for big parties. You should see it when we have guests, with lamps in all the windows and lanterns over the verandah and all the way down to the dock! It's all so lively and jolly ... boats coming and going, sometimes all the way from Sweden."

Frida nodded eagerly. She looked almost frightened.

What in the world's come over me? Am I trying to impress her? So stupid ...

"It's cold out here," Maria said. "Come on, let's go in. You've had a long trip."

Of course I could have picked her up in the car. But why? She would only have been embarrassed.

A fire was burning in the fireplace. Some lamps were lit in the early dusk, shaded circles of light making the room's colours soft and warm. The low table covered with bottles and glasses stood in front of the fire. Frida stopped in the doorway and looked around in silence. She took several steps and paused by a vase of yellow roses. "Flowers," she said. "I should have brought flowers. I thought of it, but then ..." Her voice sank and trailed away.

Maria studied her, fascinated. "I'll show you your room," she said. "You'll want to hang up your clothes. Then we'll have a drink before dinner."

♦♦♦

Maria Mickelson was an accomplished hostess, accustomed to filling pauses in the conversation. She did it spontaneously, without the least effort. Her guest ate very little. She listened with her eyes fixed on Maria's face, and gradually her smile came back and her stiff posture grew more relaxed. She no longer resembled Ellen quite so much. Maria noticed this and went quiet, a politely challenging silence. Let it be quiet – she'll just have to manage on her own. I've talked enough.

It had started to rain outside, and the rain rustled softly on the metal roof. Maria waited. She saw Frida shrink and grow anxious, fumble with her food, search desperately for something to say. Finally it came, quickly and too loud. "I saw you in your last play."

"Yes?"

"You were wonderful. Your acting is so ... natural."

"Do you think so?"

"Yes, I do."

"That's so nice to hear," Maria said and let the silence fall again.

Frida's face was red. She picked up her wineglass and took a big drink, her hand shaking.

I need to remember that her back is straight while her shoulders are thrust forward and upward. And that movement of her neck, as if her collar were choking her. That will be good. She asked, mercifully, "Do you go the theatre often?"

"Yes," Frida answered. "But mostly when you're in the play." The smile again. A great, sincere admiration. It was hard not to like cousin Frida. Of course she was very irritating and would be a catastrophe combined with other guests, but there was something about her that was very disarming, something that had been frightened into hiding and become almost invisible. It peeked out only in her smile.

After dinner, she wanted to do the dishes. She insisted, pleaded, and, when Maria finally gave in, her gratitude was almost embarrassing. Cousin Frida changed completely as soon as she had something to do. She moved quickly, calmly, matter-of-factly in the unfamiliar kitchen and in an odd way seemed to find everything she needed.

"It will be such fun to help out," she said. "I'm a good cook. And I love laying fires and getting them to burn with *one* match. I get up early in the mornings. Do you prefer coffee or tea?"

Maria sat on the firewood box and smoked. The kitchen had suddenly changed; become friendly and secure.

"Just think, here I am in the country," Frida said. "And with you. I never dreamed. It's all such an adventure."

♦♦♦

Later that evening, when Maria was alone in her room, she took out a notebook and wrote a couple of pages. She tried to remember every nuance of gesture and voice, every glance, every pause. She rehearsed them in the mirror. They worked. They'd be perfect. The hand that covered the mouth, the taut neck ... She tried to borrow Frida's smile, but without success. Her smile was entirely her own.

♦♦♦

Letting Frida take charge of the house had been a mistake. She resembled Ellen less and less. She escaped her mute helplessness by chatting about domestic details, always in motion, arranging, preparing dinners, sweeping pine needles from the verandah, raking leaves, polishing pots, carrying wood. And every time she had accomplished something and came to report, there was that

brown canine gaze, submissive but expectant. Cousin
Frida awaited praise. Maria had no use for her any longer.
After a couple of days she called Hans and asked him to
send out Mrs. Hermanson. "I know," Maria said. "She
wasn't supposed to come until later. But I need a little
help around the house. Can't you eat out this week?"

"I suppose I can," said Hans, who was a kind man.
"How's it going with your cousin?"

"Good," Maria said. "Inviting her was a good idea."

Mrs. Hermanson arrived and took over the kitchen,
the fireplaces, the cleaning, everything. And Frida crept
back into the role ordained for her. In the evenings, they
sat in front of the fire and Maria was very quiet. She
watched her cousin.

"I happened to think of something," Frida said. "Do
you have anything that needs fixing?"

"No, I don't think so."

"Well, I just thought ... The fog hasn't let up."

"No."

"Maybe I shouldn't ask," Frida said, very quietly, "but
are you working on a part right at the moment? I mean,
a new play ...?"

"Yes," Maria said. "There's a part coming up in the
autumn. A leading role."

"Oh. That's your first real lead."

"I suppose," said Maria, growing annoyed. "If you
like." She leaned forward and stirred the fire. "How did
you know that?" she asked over her shoulder.

Frida didn't answer right away; she was frightened. After
a while she said, "I clip all the stories about you. And it

seems to me the parts they give you are too small. And they don't write what they should. They really don't."

Maria stood up and walked over to the drinks table. She poured herself a drink and drank it standing, staring at the rainy verandah windows.

"Did I say something wrong?" said Frida, her voice barely audible.

"How so?" Maria walked back to the fire, her voice very chilly. She was suddenly tired of her experiment. "I just can't understand," she said. "I just can't understand why Hans wants to keep this pile of a house. It's so utterly boring. And the evenings are worst."

Frida crept up in her chair.

That's good. Let her think it's all her fault. Just like Ellen. In the second act, when she doesn't even understand that they're being mean to her ...

Maria sat down slowly and stretched her hands towards the fire. "Of course," she said, "of course I could get him to sell the place and buy something smaller and more modern, closer to town. But I think maybe my conscience would bother me ..." She turned quickly to Frida and said, "Do you ever have a bad conscience?"

"Oh yes." Her answer was hardly more than a sigh.

"Often?"

"I don't know ... Maybe all the time. Somehow ..." Her hands were folded over her stomach as if she were in pain, her chin down, her face rigid and turned away.

"But you're such a nice person. What can you possibly have done to give you a bad conscience?"

"That's just it," Frida said. She'd gone pale. "I've never done a thing, nothing at all, nothing one way or the other."

"Why not?" Maria stared at her intently.

"Maybe I never dared ... I don't know ..."

Mrs. Hermanson came in and drew the curtains, locked the verandah door, and said good night. They heard her steps in the kitchen and doors closing. Maria poured a little glass of straight whisky. "Take this," she said. "Drink it straight down like medicine. You'll feel better."

Frida stared at the glass, reached out her hand, and suddenly began to cry in long, laboured sobs. "Forgive me," she sobbed. "This is just terrible ... I'm so embarrassed ... But you're so kind, I don't understand how you can be so nice to me ..."

Maria waited, her face expressionless. When the attack had passed, she said, "Now drink that down. And then we'll go to bed. You're tired, that's all. Take an aspirin before you go to sleep."

♦♦♦

The fog had lifted and the summer night was now a deep blue. Maria lay in bed reading slowly through her script. With great care she read through cousin Frida's lines and brought them to life, one after another, with relentless attention to detail. It was a good part, very good. But it was difficult. It was only now she understood that the woman she was to play was not only submissive and insignificant; she also possessed a quality people seldom call by name – natural goodness. The quality that filled Frida's smile but that she had never been allowed to pour forth – a confined and strangled generosity.

But how does cousin Frida live? What does she do? I know nothing about her ...

Maria's thoughts began to wander, and she set the script aside. At once, the silence in the house tightened around her and in vague unease she got up and opened the door to the stairs. No streak of light under the guest room door. Frida was asleep. Or was she lying awake weeping? Maria walked to the door and listened. No, nothing. It was a relief.

Too bad, actually, that she had felt it necessary to call for Mrs. Hermanson. Well, well. She could ask cousin Frida to mend some sheets. Not tomorrow, maybe. But soon. And maybe tell her some stories, some theatre stories. Everyone always seemed to like those.

The Locomotive

WHAT I AM ABOUT TO WRITE may seem exaggerated, but the cornerstone of what I have to relate is really my single-minded devotion to objectivity. In truth, I am not telling a story, I am recounting facts. I am known for my detachment and precision. And what I am trying to convey is intended for me alone, to help me make sense of certain events.

This is difficult to write, I don't know where to begin. Perhaps with some facts. I am an expert mechanical draughtsman and have worked for United Railways all my life. My drawings are very precise and skilful. For many years I have also acted as a secretary – a subject I will return to. My story has a great deal to do with locomotives.

(I am fond of lovely old words like "locomotive".) Naturally I often draw details of this particular machine as a part of my job, and in doing this work I am a model of calm, professional pride, but in the evenings, when I come home to my apartment, I draw machines in motion, locomotives in particular. I do this for my amusement. It is a hobby, not to be confused with an ambition. Over the last few years, I have drawn and coloured a whole series of such illustrations and sometimes I think they could be made into a book. But I am not finished yet and won't be for a long time to come. When I retire, I intend to devote all of my time to the locomotive, or, rather, to the idea of the locomotive. At the moment, I am forced to write, every day, in order to clarify this. The drawings are not enough.

A very long time ago, I used to walk to school by way of the railway terminal. It was a long walk, and I seem to remember that it was always terribly cold, but I walked as slowly as I could because that route was the best and most vivid part of my entire day. I told myself stories. And when I got to the warmth of the railway terminal I would often finish off a chapter right then and there. That is, I would save a high point, an unbearably exciting moment, for the minutes I would linger at the entrance to the platforms with the locomotives before my very eyes. Then I would let it happen.

They were enormous, coal black, trimmed in brass, green and red. Sometimes they would roll in with a screech in a thick plume of smoke, or they would glide slowly away from the platform, gathering strength and gaining speed, pistons working like great muscles. That was beautiful. Or they would just stand there breathing their white breath into the winter cold, panting with exhaustion and satisfaction after their long journeys. They had a wonderful strength, but they were tired. Nowadays, engines carry no fire in their bellies.

Obviously – it's important to point this out – obviously I could have taken the trolley to school, and of course I had good, warm, well-made clothing. I was not badly treated either at school or at home. But when I try to remember, I recall no other reality than those long walks, telling myself stories with an excitement that reached its climax at the railway terminal. Sometimes I was the engineer, driving thousands of helpless people through the night, increasing the speed, stoking the fire like a madman, blowing the whistle, the passengers growing increasingly alarmed, stumbling through the violently shaking cars to find the conductor, shouting, "What's wrong? What's happened?" And the conductor, pale as a ghost, answering, "God help us all, the machine is out of control, something has happened to the brakes ..."

Sometimes I was a ship's captain, and I'd let the steamer brush against a reef, an iceberg, and everything and everyone on board would quake with fear for one long, anxious second and then, with a dreadful grating sound like that of tearing metal, the ship would continue on its way. But for how long? Only I knew. I was the emperor, with the power of life and death. I closed schools, I forbade entire populations to bear children. It was a splendid game – one game in the morning on the way to school and another on the way home. Everything else passed unnoticed, like time, and I remember very little. But my games gradually grew more refined and, at the same time, simpler. No one knew who I was – that was tremendously important. They never guessed who it was that walked among them, doing the same things they did at the same times of the day. How strong I must have been. I will write no more today.

Later. I have a very nice apartment – living room, bedroom, kitchen, bathroom and work room. In the work room I've had shelves built for my illustrations, but it is in no sense an atelier – I must emphasize that point. It is, rather, a professional library. The word "atelier" unavoidably conveys an impression of picturesque romantic squalor. Nothing could be more alien to me. But a work room is simply a room where a person works, a space for a person's vocational materials. I have never shown anyone my locomotive art.

I eat out but make my own tea in the mornings and evenings. My apartment is very quiet. Sometimes when I'm having my evening tea I get the odd feeling that I don't exist, almost as if I had never existed. This is one of those details that writing may help me to explain. I need to write every day and I must always take great pains to be precise. For that matter, it is a part of my job. I have been accused of being standoffish, of never showing my face. This has happened several times. But what gives them the right to see my face? I don't know what they expect of me, but, whatever it is, they have no right to it.

Later. Perhaps I should use the third person singular instead. "He" is more objective than "I". It seems to me.

So, he had never shown anyone his locomotive art. In his job as secretary and technical draughtsman (I am now repeating myself, but I do so intentionally) at United Railways, at professional conferences, when delivering drawings, at lunches, etc., he came into contact with quite a few people, often people who talked openly and seemed to be in no hurry. He soon noticed that, unlike himself, they revealed themselves freely. He gradually discovered that he could make use of their openness. Afterwards, when he came home to his apartment and continued with the work he called his own – the locomotive illustrations – he found it easier to depict the strength, the motion, the sovereign power of the machine.

At home, of course, he never received visitors. The apartment was utterly his own.

In the beginning, he just listened, very attentively. Later he learned to ask the right questions, to entice his interlocutors to speak of what mattered to them most in the world. This was not usually difficult, especially at a lunch or an office party. He waited patiently. He probed his way forward with questions and very soon arrived at what they really cared about, what they hoped for or feared. With infinite care, he led them on. It was a kind of game or, shall we say, a hobby. And quite a splendid source of material. "The locomotive principle" was what he called the moment when they revealed themselves. As they approached that revelation, he observed carefully their faces and hands, their voices and pauses, all of which, much more than their words, gave an impression of restrained power – and that was just what he needed for his work. The inherent, restrained power of the machine. For that matter, faces – and especially hands – had always seemed to him painfully naked. Another indicator, even more unconscious, is body language, especially the back and the neck. One time outside a shop, I caught sight of myself in a treacherously positioned double mirror, in semi-profile, from behind. It was very unpleasant.

I'm getting off the subject. Wait.

He made use of their intensity regardless of where it was concentrated, sometimes in the most ridiculous hopes and propensities. He collected their energy, went home, and could often work for hours on his conception of the consummate machine. He loved machines, their power, their perfection, their supreme indifference. While people chatted their way to their manias or, let us say, to their motive power, he was very careful not to be drawn into any kind of relationship. He did draw nearer to them, but evasively, and he never sought to converse with women. There were people who retreated afterwards, but he had already used them. Now I'm tired. I'll continue later.

There were dangerous people and unreachable people, but there were also the confused, the innocent, the manic, and those who were friendly because they were helpless. On the whole, so much power goes to waste! Naturally, categories are always simplified concepts. In the case of human beings they are perhaps as readily distinguishable as, say, the few recurring nightmares that haunt their sleep. (I will return later to the question of dreams, in particular the one about the locomotive. Am I including too much detail? There is much of this I should delete.)

Another day. Sometimes I become unreasonably tired in the evenings. I put my work aside because I cannot draw the full-fledged machine and at the same time make it move, rush, dash, plunge forward, and my head feels like a lump of iron, gliding out of my reach. But most tired of all are my hands. They lie beside me as heavy as the earth, sinking deeper and deeper.

I don't like taking people by the hand. The expression "a helping hand" is disagreeable. Why should I

I have lost my train of thought.

New section:

Sometimes, when he was listening to people, he pretended that they were about to travel – always by train. They begin with small talk, tiny things, the way you do just before the train departs, carelessly, hastily. But the moment the train starts to move, they blurt out what's important to them, the crucial, irrevocable revelation, like a postscript at the end of an irreproachably cautious letter.

And so they vanished, he allowed them to vanish, and he drew away – safely back onto the platform as it slipped rapidly backwards – and went home to work.

Oh stifled power, unleashed in a release of steam, the splendid locomotive of my youth with its long howl, all expectation and alarm, rising straight to the sooty cupolas of every railway shed. The pistons begin to move and then, majestically, dragging its cars in its wake, the locomotive leaves behind on the dreary platform everything that can be left behind and everyone who has said too much or managed to say nothing at all! It is thee I attempt to portray!

I need to revise this, too personal. Check.

Delete or explain why. But I don't know why.

A locomotive dragging all the world's unease back and forth across the whole face of the earth could grow very tired.

Note: I have always been extremely wary of women. They are undependable.

Later.

Sometimes he played with the idea of focusing on one traveller – a *Traveller*, that beautiful, old-fashioned word – and attach himself ever so lightly and with no strings to someone about to undertake a long journey. It could be the pure, free starting gate to an attachment, a longing that need never become contaminated or come too close. The thudding of the rails is like a heartbeat, a rhythmic pulse in the stomach and gut, further down, further away, finally only a vibration, the rails are empty and clean, then silence and liberation.

He had never ridden a train. Had no desire to do so.

Actual experience can never be the same as imagined experience. So he believed.

Railway terminal is another lovely, dignified expression. Now, in middle age, he often passed the terminal and would linger for a moment. But at night – and here are the recurring dreams – at night he would dream about the real locomotives. He was in a hurry, a great hurry, the train was about to leave and he wasn't packed, he couldn't find his passport and didn't know his destination, but it was important, painfully important, and he ran from track to track and had forgotten which train he was supposed to take and when it left and from which platform ... It was too late, it was all too late. The only person who had ever noticed that he existed was going away never to return, the only person he had not despised and who did not fit into any category. The locomotive screamed, shrieked, and he jumped between the tracks and, with a great metallic roar, the locomotive came closer and closer and drowned and crushed him in its boundless grandeur. He grabbed convulsively at a handle and the air that howled around him was hot, monstrously hot ...

I know that others also dream about trains, but not the way I do, not at all. They are only afraid of missing the train, simply that. They don't feel the pain I feel.

I will try to explain my illustrations. I gather all the strong colours in the locomotive – deep Prussian blue, coal black, and in the black hints of red and white fire, the machine's splendid wide-open eyes that nevertheless carry no hint of threat, the locomotive is utterly indifferent to whatever comes in its path and to everything that coils along behind it, those anonymous cars forever filling and emptying and filling again, of no interest whatsoever, like women.

I have now read through what I've written. I wonder if it is sufficiently straightforward or perhaps, on the contrary, overly explicit. I have been criticized for giving too much attention to detail, but that is precisely what makes me such a good secretary. A long life has taught me to notice and value facts, and I seldom make a mistake. I will now try to continue.

His locomotive studies were done in watercolour, black India ink, and the transparent, luminous Bengali ink that's used for colouring photographs. Of course, he realized he was not the only artist to see into the soul of the locomotive. The painter Turner has quite convincingly represented their dizzying speed and power, but he conceals what we might call the face of the locomotive in steam and fog. We understand, but we do not see. I find his painting of the onrushing train very depressing. He shows us not the locomotive but only himself.

I'll wait until tomorrow. I won't continue at the moment.

It was a Sunday. He got up very late and sat down at his work table. He didn't like easels, because his hands and arms grew so heavy that he needed the table's support. Letting your head sink onto your arms for a moment doesn't count, no more than those quick half-dreams that punctuate a sleepless night. He spoiled an important surface that couldn't be redone, neither with water, a razor blade, nor by painting over. He sat quietly for a while and stared at his drawing, then he put on his overcoat and walked to the railway terminal. To this day he went there when he felt distressed. Several trains were in, but he paid them no attention. He went to the restaurant and had a beer. The place was full, perfect strangers were sharing tables, trying to look past the people across from them or stare down into their plates. They ate hastily and had placed their bags and suitcases tightly under the legs of their tables. It was crowded and the smell of food was stronger than usual. He drank his beer and despised them. He despised everything just at the moment. And his back ached, the small of his back, where it always aches when you reach an impasse. Directly across from him sat a thin woman in a black coat. She'd been eating cabbage and sausage and now she took out a cigarette and started searching for matches in her purse.

"Excuse me," she said, "but do you have a match?"

He pushed a box across to her and decided to go. "You have paint on your face," she said. Her tone was utterly matter-of-fact, as if she had said your suitcase is open or you have a wasp on your coat, and her gaze moved on at once and she didn't smile. Her discretion was unusual for a woman, and to show his appreciation he asked politely where she was off to. "Nowhere," she said. "I don't like to travel." And a few moments later, as if she thought her reply had been a bit brusque, she added, "I just come here sometimes to look at the trains."

He grew attentive, alert as a hunter. He asked why she was interested in trains, in what way, and had she really never travelled? No, she just liked to look at trains.

Earlier, when he was trying to uncover people's innermost essence, he had never sought out women. It was possible, even probable, that they could have given him even more usable material, but sound instinct warned him off. Women can exact a heavy price for a confidence and it was best to avoid them. Now he studied this woman who came to the railway terminal solely and exclusively because she wanted to watch the trains come and go, and he thought, is it possible, have I finally met someone I can talk to and who will understand?

"You are fascinated by the locomotives, am I right?" he said.

She shrugged her shoulders and said, "I don't really know. It's simply the trains. You know, the trains."

She was a perfectly ordinary woman, maybe a little over forty. Nothing but her interest distinguished her from the others, except perhaps her heavy eyebrows. Now she put out her cigarette and rose to leave. With a little nod to him, she made her way among the chairs of all the other diners and walked out into the waiting room, a strikingly tall and angular creature. She reminded him of a crow.

He thought about her for a long time afterwards. He had never before met anyone obsessed with trains in principle, only people whose jobs involved the railroad or who insisted on talking about their travels. In this woman's case, it was clearly not a question of the locomotive but rather of the cars, a natural feminine perception – to follow, to accept, to be as it were swept along. Another important detail – she had never wanted to travel. What captivated her was not the banal desire to seek out warmer and lovelier climes, an easier or more exciting life, no, she loved trains as such, as a phenomenon. Did she see the beauty of the train? Did she fantasize about a train trip's freedom from responsibility? Setting forth, out, away ... And as you are carried off, everything you leave behind becomes irreparable, final, and what you're approaching has not yet made its claims. You are a Traveller. For a short time, you are free.

It seemed to him terribly important that he should speak to her. He returned to the railway terminal almost every day, but she wasn't there. He tried to remember her face, but all he remembered were her unplucked eyebrows and that she was tall and thin and wore black. The winter continued cold. He worked on his drawings in the evenings. He decided to paint people in the train windows, but he didn't like the result and washed them off. He saw people at the office but he no longer tried to get them to talk about themselves, and he walked past the terminal less and less frequently. But his thoughts returned again and again to the woman who liked trains. She became a game. He gave her qualities, character-istics, experiences, a profession, even a childhood. He made her strong, brave and mysterious. It was the first time in his conscious life that he had taken an interest in another human being.

One evening he could not go on working. He had reached a highly critical point. What remained to be added was so important, so delicate, that he needed to pause. I have never been able to decide whether those final, decisive lines or brushstrokes should be done with concentrated intensity or perhaps just the opposite, on sudden impulse, feverishly. I don't know. One can destroy so much or gain you never know what – but there is nothing of the gambler in me. My principle has always been to feel my way. I'm always searching, and time passes, so very soon I have no more time. Strange, is it not, that the locomotive should be the motive force (ha ha) for this artist?

Wait a moment.

He went out – to the railway terminal. And there she stood on the platform. She was taller than all the other people waiting there, but what primarily set her apart from the crowd were her shoulders and the way she held her head, an immobility that showed she was not there to meet someone, that she was waiting only for the train. It came in, slowed, stopped, the platform filled with people hurrying towards one another or past one another, but she didn't move. When the platform around her was nearly empty, she turned to go. Then he walked up and asked her if she recognized him. She nodded. Her expression was rather sharp, and for a moment he was confused by the fact that her face didn't match the picture of her he had created in his imagination. Only her eyebrows were the same, very thick and dark, while beneath them her eyes seemed oddly uncertain. She looked away.

"You needn't be uneasy," he said. "I would just like to talk to you, talk about trains, about traveling ..."

"I've never travelled," she said.

So he tried to explain. "That's why I must talk with you. I don't travel either, but I'm fascinated by trains, just as you are ..."

She started walking towards the waiting room. She didn't understand. It was a ridiculous situation. She had long legs and walked very quickly, he almost had to run to keep up.

"Just for a little while," he begged. "You wouldn't like a cup of coffee? No? But we could sit in the waiting room, if you have time. Surely you can spare a few minutes?"

They sat down on a bench and she lit a cigarette. Naturally, he had imagined an easy conversation comparing their views on the symbolism of travel and trains, absolutely nothing personal, but her compact silence, the feeling that she might at any moment stand up and go, made him lose his footing. For the first time in his life, he grew careless and revealed himself. He told her about his drawings, about his dream of one day finishing them and getting them published as a book. He told her what trains had meant to him when he was young ... Occasionally he stopped and waited, but the woman beside him went on smoking and said nothing. And finally, driven by her silence, he humiliated himself by telling her of the anguished dreams in which he kept missing trains. He talked faster and faster, unable to stop himself. All this time, people were carrying their bags back and forth right in front of them, and the loudspeakers were calling out train arrivals and departures, so he raised his voice and tried to force her to look at him, and then finally he took her hand and cried, "Do you see? Do you see what I mean? This is serious for me, it's important. You must think I'm crazy, but if you saw my drawings you'd understand that I really know what I'm talking about and that I'm perfectly lucid – in fact, I'm practically a scholar on the subject."

"I understand," said the woman, solemnly. "I understand what you mean." She seemed to be searching for words in the same aimless way that she was always digging around in her purse. Finally she simply repeated, "I understand."

He was very tired. They went into the restaurant.

Now, afterwards, it seems incredible that I didn't grasp what that meant. When a woman says that she understands, it means quite simply and simplistically that she's getting away with as little effort as possible. She, this special woman, couldn't find the words because she had nothing to say. But I, who had spent such a long time fashioning her character and giving her particular qualities, I saw in her silence merely reticent strength, an independence that that allowed no one to come too close. It's incomprehensible.

Later.

She's coming tomorrow, so I won't be able to work, I will only be aware that she is here in the apartment. But before she comes, there are many things I need to clarify. I need to go through what I've written and spell things out in greater detail. But not right now.

Watch out for repeated words.

He had hired her to keep house for him. She was to come three times a week to cook, clean, etc. The woman's name was Anna, so let us call her simply Anna (a name as pale as milk). Why did he do it? It's unbelievable. Why had he let her in? Was it because she, this woman, Anna, was the only person who knew him? She was therefore important and needed to be kept close? Was that how it happened?

The first time she came she was wearing a white apron under her coat and carried a bag apparently containing what she would need for her housework. She was very correct and asked to go directly to the kitchen. But since Anna – I will try to use her name, although I prefer to think of her as "the woman" – since Anna had now become the person closest to me personally,

I suggested that she look around the apartment. She followed me through my rooms, and as she earnestly and carefully observed the objects I am accustomed to having around me, I saw my rooms through her eyes as if for the first time, and they struck me as oddly empty. She said nothing. How could I know why? She was elusive, guarded, unreachable. It was, of course, for this reason that I could believe in her hidden strength for such a long time, the strength my dream had given her.

We came into my work room. Needless to say, I had put away my locomotive art. Only some mechanical drawings lay on the table. She looked at them and then at me, a kind of veiled, conspiratorial glance, and she smiled. For the first time, she smiled, but it was a frightening, intimate smirk. She had not forgotten. No, she had not forgotten my unburdening myself. And she believed that these mechanical drawings were my locomotive illustrations!

Right then and there I should have sent her away, but I did not. She continued to come, she cleaned and cooked, and the whole time I was afraid of her sudden, quiet smile and that quick conspiratorial glance. Not rapport, not the sharing of an important secret – rather the sharing of something shameful, a shame she could forgive but never take seriously.

Perhaps all my life I've needed someone who is very strong and who tells me what to do.

It wasn't she.

She wasn't even a passenger.

Now I'm very tired. I'll wait.

So, anyway she smiled and went to the kitchen. She's here every third day. I count the days by her, the woman Anna. She owns everything I have ever allowed to slip past my self-restraint, my dignity, my private autonomy.

One moment. I'm writing too quickly. I've lost the thread again.

So, he tried to put her in her place, but she kept avoiding him, and now and then, as she swept by, she'd give him that horrible smile, that smirk of shameful collusion. But then her eyes looked away again. She never stood behind that smile.

I had thought that I'd finally found a traveller, a person who travelled in her thoughts, in her dreams, at home in her room, much more than those who perpetually criss-cross the globe. I thought she might have understood my great catastrophes that never put anyone at risk but that did get people to notice me, to see that I existed and that it was I who had saved them. I could have shown her my locomotive drawings. But I waited. I no longer trusted her.

We used to take our meals together, and she would take off her apron to eat with me.

I was on edge the whole time, perhaps with anticipation, perhaps with fear. I still didn't know if the woman Anna had brought my dream vision closer – or destroyed it. It was impossible to speak to her, not only because her vocabulary was unusually limited but also because I was never sure if she understood me. And yet I could not keep quiet, I babbled endlessly, helplessly. I was sometimes gripped by an overwhelming need to take back everything I'd said, deny it, erase it, but even stronger was the compulsion to confide still more in her, to give her details, to shower her with everything that had been and could have been my life. I would follow her out to the kitchen and talk and talk about myself, leaning against the counter, at the kitchen table, I could not stop! And when I had finally crucified myself, she would smile and want to go for a walk. She insisted on helping me on with my overcoat and made sure I hadn't forgotten my scarf. She owned me, she had swallowed me. She was a kind of monster, believe me, a monster. We always walked to the railway terminal, and when the evening train glided in to the platform, she would take my hand and press it conspiratorially, and every time an odd warmth would run through me, violent, as strong as when I was young and saw trains come in and felt that now I'd forget the brakes and drive the locomotive straight in over the platform and the people, straight in!

Delete later

I am often very tired lately, though I don't work more than necessary. Have I managed to explain everything that happened? Or am I being tedious? I need to go over all of this very carefully.

One mild Sunday in late winter, she suggested that we go to the botanical gardens instead of the railway terminal. Why? Well, because the woman Anna liked greenhouses. We went. And as we stood there in the humid, overheated glass building contemplating the static greenery, she took my hand the same way she was in the habit of doing when a train came in. She pressed my hand and gave me that ghastly smile. We returned home. We walked side by side, and I knew that the woman beside me carried with her everything that was me and that it had no effect on her whatsoever and that she had understood nothing.

We continued with our daily lives along quiet paths of repetition and accommodation, paths we wore steadily deeper. Try to imagine a track, a furrow that gradually wears its way so deep that one can no longer climb out over the edges, only continue, continue walking, running, dashing in the same direction ... I began to hate her. Not immediately. But instead of ignoring her, forgetting that she existed, I was conscious of her every second of my waking life, and at night she ravaged my dreams. What was I waiting for? There was no longer anything to wait for, there was nothing for us to share except those meals, during which I usually read, and her abominable walks. Every day I decided to fire the woman Anna, very politely, give her a large sum of money; every day I decided at least to be silent, to say nothing; and every day was a miserable failure. In the end I was driven irrevocably to show her my own work, the careening locomotive.

"But where is the platform?" she asked. "Isn't the train in the station?" And I saw, through her terrible, stupid eyes, I saw that the locomotive was standing still. It was not moving. I turned the picture to the wall and went to the window so I wouldn't have to look at her. The room was silent for several minutes. The she came up to me from behind and put her arms around me. For a moment, her long, hot body was pressed against mine. It was hideous. She said something. I don't know what she said. I don't know what happened except that I suddenly ran down the street to the corner where I buy my newspaper.

Did I mention that spring was on the way?

I'm not an experienced writer, but I need to finish this story. The woman Anna began calling me by my first name. My nightly dreams changed. It was no longer the locomotive that haunted me, it was she. As always, I was running across the tracks with the terminal's massive glass-and-metal skeleton against the night sky above me, and far off I heard trains whistling on their way to distant places, but now she came leaping towards me over the tracks like some black bird. She was hot and smelled of sweat and held her arms wide to catch me, and at the same time I knew that she already had me, had every-thing that was me stowed away in her belly, undigested and irredeemable. I awoke in unspeakable terror and my first thought was, is it today she's coming? Is it today or not until tomorrow ...?

Her days off came to be the most difficult. I could not stop thinking about her for a second, and my hatred seemed almost unbearable. I was bound to her the way a person is linked to a conscience, a shadow, a crime. She was never unfriendly towards me. As I sat at my mechanical drawings, she might put down a plate beside me – she had baked something, made pastries of some kind – or a cup of coffee or some flowers in a glass. She emptied my ashtray and went out into the kitchen and closed the door so quietly that it made the hair stand up on the back of my neck.

I began having different dreams. I dreamed that I turned on her and screamed with hate and raised my hands to heaven and chased her with intent to kill. She was the one running away across the tracks, she was the one panting and stumbling and looking back over her shoulder, screaming when she saw me coming after her with hands like claws! And I woke up, sobbing. I was strangling the sheets.

Anna bought vitamins for me. She didn't think I looked healthy, thought I was pale and ought to rest or take a trip. She actually said "take a trip". A little later she added, "Why, we could take a little trip together." I said nothing and let her prattle on about Mallorca and the Canary Islands, group travel, how much she had saved and how she would be no trouble. And if I didn't want to fly, a trip by train could be just as much fun – we could go north instead, maybe Rovaniemi, where they have such a nice hotel with reindeer hides and a big fireplace ... She wanted to treat me. She actually wanted to treat me to the trip, and finally she said, "Why, I'll bet it would be nice for you, since you're so interested in trains."

I think that was the day I decided that she would die.

I prepared for the trip very carefully, reserved sleeping-car accommodation well in advance, booked rooms at the hotel in Rovaniemi. I walked around as if in a friendly haze, everything dulled and shapeless, and it felt wonderful. The woman Anna was garrulous with pleasure, proclaiming again and again how right it was that the two of us, who had never travelled, should make this journey together. She baked pirogies, she put together a lunch to eat on the train, she was secretive and painfully roguish. I went out into the kitchen looking for matches and saw a bowl of blood on the counter, yes, blood, somewhat coagulated, with foam around the edges. She said it was for blood pancakes – we could eat them cold with lingonberry jam. On the night train. She'd worked it all out.

That bowl of blood was horrible. I felt ill and left the room, closed the door on her, and I thought, I can't do it, I can't stand the sight of it. But we can stand more than we think, and everything must proceed to its logical conclusion. There are times when only ideas and a strong will are equal to the task before us ...

Wait, I'm digressing, but I can fix that later. Right now I just need to go on writing as fast as I can, so we came to the railway terminal and I helped her up with all our bags and baskets and bought a carnation she wanted to pin on her coat and magazines and asked if she wanted a Coca-Cola or some juice and all the while the locomotive stood quietly waiting for me and the hands of the platform clock moved ahead in little jerks, every minute a little jerk, and then she cried, "Oh if only there was someone to see us off, someone to wish us a pleasant journey!" And when the train began to glide along the rails, she leaned out, holding the handle of the door, and waved and waved at people she didn't know and leaned further and further out as they slipped back and away and my locomotive was already picking up speed and as the wind began to grab at her I gave the door a shove – the impact ran through me like a flame – and the door swung out and she went with it and vanished in a flicker of black, a fluttering bird. That's all there was to it.

I had thought through the whole thing so often and so meticulously that every detail was polished, every possibility taken into account. At first I had the locomotive whistle, a long cry as she fell, but I took that out. Another possibility was to have the woman go into the compartment to organize the baggage and the pillows, presumably waving out the window when the train started to move so she couldn't see when I jumped off on the other side. But my attention to detail was insurmountable – the doors on that side are locked. Then I decided to go and buy cigarettes at the last minute, a perfectly natural thing to do. She stands in the window uneasily and sees me running and calls out, "Hurry! Hurry! The train's leaving!" But it's too late. I slow down, I spread my arms in helpless resignation.

I could also have waved to her and laughed. But that would have been almost too cruel.

Flower Child

WHEN FLORA JOHANSSON was young, she was often compared to a flower, and she wore her floral name with an adorable self-consciousness. A slender neck, billowy straw-coloured hair, and great flower-blue eyes whose steady gaze might have seemed steely had it not been veiled by long, carefully mascaraed lashes. She dressed her slim body in a touchingly childish but deliberate manner, often in a skirt and girlish blouse with rounded collars like the petals of a flower. Concealed behind these small, stiff uniforms, her feminine wiles seemed charming but also a little disturbing. The men who slept with her had the feeling of having seduced a schoolgirl. Flora Johansson spoke of her love affairs with disarming naiveté. It was as if she were telling anecdotes about devoted pets, all of whom were deserving of equal, fair and simultaneous attention. There was a matter-of-fact amorality about her, the way a marsh cradles a waterlily but leaves it unsullied.

Flora's father worked in public relations for a rubber company, a large heavy man, as ugly as his wife. They spoiled Flora, presumably because they never recovered from their astonishment at having produced such a beautiful daughter. Flora's friends were like her, members of the same privileged clan of ease and pleasure. At one time or another, they had all slept with each other – borrowed, exchanged or stolen each other's partners – and had as a result become unusually tolerant, a quality they took great pride in. At the same time, they could not avoid occasionally playing games with the truth. The pleasures of love were freed from any serious pathos but also deprived of natural shyness and charm.

When Flora was twenty-two, she suddenly married an American named John Vogelsong, one of her father's business contacts in rubber. There were a lot of good jokes about this Vogelsong. Among other things, her friends said that Flora had simply fallen in love with his name as a kind of complement to her own flowery appellation. For the wedding, her friends composed witty verses based on Flora's new name and its associations, high-spirited verses that naturally included references to the rubber industry and, in innocently obscene form, suggested the bride's brief but comprehensive emotional life prior to her change of name. The verses were not translated for John Vogelsong, a friendly mediocrity who looked a little tired. His morning gift to Flora was a necklace of diamonds and sapphires. Sapphires highlighted Flora's eyes in an altogether exceptional way. The next morning, the newlyweds flew off to Bali, where the groom planned to combine a short honeymoon with a little business, whereupon they would return to his house outside Los Angeles, California.

In the beginning, there were quite a few letters from Flora, to her parents and above all to her friends. She wrote rapturous descriptions of her new home, garden, swimming pool, yacht, and the unbelievable parties at which almost all the guests were famous for one reason or another. All if it was almost too good to be true! As time went by, she wrote less often. Her friends no longer received separate letters but a single one in common. John worked too much and had some kind of stomach problem. "Darlings, all you dear children, how I wish all of you could be here to cheer up my big, tired businessman, the poor dear. There's not much birdsong for him in LA. Business, business, business ... If only you could all fly in and shower him with rainbows and bouquets of the gaiety he needs! God, how I miss you! He travels almost constantly ... And he doesn't even have fun in all the wonderful places he visits. He hardly has time to see them. Now, if it was *me*...!!"

Eventually, Flora's letters stopped. There came a time when she sent pretty postcards from different parts of the world. Sometimes the card was a photograph – Flora in a bikini on a beach, Flora in a topee on a camel or on a horse in an equestrian helmet. Each card was signed with a flower, happy and blooming or wilting, expectantly in bud form or with withered leaves and a guilty expression and sometimes viewed by a ruffled bird with various facial expressions. "Boys and girls, this is the life! Never a dull moment. It's simply *fabulous*!" Flora's friends replied in the same style with drawings of flowers and birds, disrespectful and affectionate arabesques, by and by almost without any text. "We're sitting here drinking white wine in the sunshine and thinking of you, you wicked flower child who has abandoned us!" And signed with all of their names. In the end it was only Papa and Mama who heard from Flora, each time with the vague promise of a visit. "Just think what fun ... You really must come out here ... Next time John goes to Scandinavia ..."

But, before John could come to Scandinavia, the war broke out. And, before the war was over, Papa and Mama had died.

◆◆◆

Thirty-four years after Flora became Mrs Vogelsong, the world she had grown accustomed to collapsed. The tired John Vogelsong was found dead in his bed and in the classic letter on the night table he reported concisely that he was ruined and begged Flora's forgiveness. Since he had had never burdened his wife with information about his work (work that in any case would not have interested her and that she wouldn't have understood), he now mentioned in a postscript that she need do nothing but call Shoon & Shoon, to whom he had given instructions with regard to certain arrangements. These turned out to be a bank deposit, not exactly overwhelming, and a small apartment in San Pedro. It was really very small, and the blue ocean outside the window did nothing but make Flora feel even lonelier and sadder. She was still flowerlike – though now, perhaps, more like a slightly dusty everlasting – and her girlishness had acquired a touch of anxiety, of which she was naturally unaware.

After two months in San Pedro, Flora decided to go home. Shoon & Shoon sold her apartment and made arrangements for her trip down to the last detail. Her furniture would follow later. "You understand, my dear Mr. Shoon," Flora explained, "that I am completely impractical! And believe it or not, I am at my absolute worst when it comes to money. Numbers! I quite simply have no head for figures. Isn't that terrible?" She cocked her head to one side and smiled. "I'm a hopeless creature and I know it."

Flora wrote to her friends and told them what had happened. "My darlings, I'm coming home! Just as in the old days, we'll sit with our white wine and toss words back and forth, long happy evenings. . . I want to know *everything* you've been up to, including your secrets! If I know you right, you won't have turned over a new leaf since last we met! Ciao. See you soon." And she drew a very wilted flower stretching its arms longingly across troubled waters.

◆◆◆

It was Helen who met her bus from the airport. They embraced, and Flora wept on Helen's shoulder. So much had happened – half a life! It was hard for them to say the customary "You haven't changed a bit ..." But Helen complimented Flora's sable fur, and Flora said, "You've changed your hair! It becomes you!" And they talked about the trip over and how dreadful the weather was. Helen explained that the others were at work and that she'd thought about coming out to the airport, but, you know, a taxi all that way ... In the taxi to the hotel, Flora got to hear all the news about deaths, divorces and grandchildren. It was all utterly unreal and made her anxious, more so than in San Pedro.

In her hotel room a bottle of white wine and a bouquet of forget-me-nots stood on the table, and Flora started to cry again. "Darlings," she sobbed. "They're my flowers, my own flowers from the old days ... I knew you wouldn't forget your Flora Vogelsong."

◆◆◆

That evening, those still available gathered in one of the hotel's private dining rooms. They drank champagne through the whole dinner and reminded each other of escapades they'd shared thirty-five years earlier. They were elated and loud. Almost every exchange began with "Do you remember?" They all toasted Flora, who had a wreath of flowers around her plate, and they all applauded when she put the wreath on her head and smiled. She couldn't see her friends all that distinctly without her glasses, but she could see colour, movement, candles, and she finally experienced a warmth and a sense of security that was a genuine homecoming and a confirmation. She wore her sapphire necklace and a long blue dress. For a moment she was afraid she was over-dressed, but then it seemed only natural that their lost flower child should come back from the other side of the world dressed like a princess. She confided this thought to them in a little roguish speech, spoke also of the loneliness that would never again oppress her and hinted at the rakish wedding verses they had written so long ago ... Suddenly reminded of her wedding and full to the brim with emotion and champagne, Flora began to snivel and sat down helplessly in the middle of a sentence. She raised her glass. "Ciao ... Children, children ... Your Flora is hopeless, isn't she? She hasn't changed a bit!"

◆◆◆

Papa's and Mama's inheritance had remained in the country, and with the help of her friends Flora found an apartment, even smaller than the one in San Pedro. With a courageous laugh, she called it her little lair, sometimes her studio. Her friends came to see her, but they never managed to recapture the extravagant mood that had carried them through her welcome-home party. Memories, questions and messages had been exhausted, and it was difficult and uncomfortable to give detailed descriptions of things that had happened in the distant past. A tight group around a tiny table presupposed an intimate contact that no longer existed. They conversed rather than chatted, and at times there was silence. Flora saw her friends more clearly at this close range, and she noticed a certain shabbiness both in dress and appearance. Oh, they were changed in so many ways! Finally she told them about her travels. They listened, they laughed, they were amazed, but their comments were monosyllabic and their questions lacked the impulsive desire to know more.

Flora tried hard and kept on trying. They were always busy, there was no end to their troubles. Jobs and health and grandchildren and finances and a host of other concerns that ruled out any chance of getting together and having fun.

"You mustn't be unhappy with us," Helen said. "We can't be the same people we were then."

"Of course not," Flora said. "It would be childish to expect you to. But all the same ... there must be *something* left, if we only try ..."

In the end she called old school friends, old fogies who could hardly remember who she was. She tried to read, but she wasn't used to it and found it made her uneasy and depressed. The people in books were unreachable, and all she got from them was an even stronger sense of life passing her by.

♦♦♦

Flora got into the habit of keeping several bottles of champagne at home. A glass or two made her happy and indifferent. And flowers, always flowers. Sometimes she didn't bother to go out and eat. She would open a bottle with that festive pop that always gave her the same sense of expectation and, reclining on her sofa, smiling, eyes half closed, she would drink toasts with the incomprehensible world that had left her in the lurch.

She discovered that champagne in the morning gave the day a promising lustre. She gradually populated her room with people she remembered or might have met, and finally she began talking to them. Not much. She welcomed them and offered them a glass of champagne. It amused her to have whispered conversations with people who came and went at her pleasure.

Flowers grew less expensive now in spring, and she could buy large bouquets. She had only to call the store around the corner. She had her champagne delivered as well, a case at a time. She avoided going out into the city, which had acquired so many new, unfamiliar buildings and was so much uglier than the cities she had seen around the world. The few times Flora saw her friends, she was distant and mysterious, a little unsteady on her legs and rather quiet. They worried about her for a while and then sent Helen to talk sense to her. Flora responded that she was happy and touched by their concern but that they shouldn't worry about their wicked flower child.

More and more, the world shrouded her in a friendly fog. It grew easier and easier to fall asleep, an hour here, several hours there; dusk and dawn and night no longer marked the implacable passage of time, and she never needed to wait. Flora Vogelsong spread her sable coat over the sofa, received her invisible guests in her blue dress and told them about her life. "When you look at me," she whispered, "you might suppose that I have always been a rather proper little wife. Oh, far from it! You don't believe me? Reclining on this sable coat, I would receive my lovers ..."

"You are so fragile," they said. "You're like a porcelain flower, one dares hardly touch you ..."

"Ciao! A little more champagne? Have you ever been in Juan les Pins? Now there's an amusing spot! They stay open all night, of course only during the season ... Suddenly someone gets an idea, everyone runs down to the beach and goes bathing in the moonlight, naked ... Or we hop in a car and barrel off to Monaco over the border, the casino never closes ... But must you really go? No, of course if you must you must. In fact I'm expecting someone, someone very special ... And maybe I'll sleep for a bit." And Flora fell asleep on her fur coat and the day passed into evening and she awoke and drank a little champagne, just one glass so she could experience everything with that much greater clarity.

A Memory from
the New World

In a large American city, Johanna from Finland sat mending underwear in the room she had rented for herself and her two younger sisters. It was a March evening, and outside in the early spring dusk the street lights came on.

It had been hard in the beginning. They had missed the silence and couldn't sleep. None of them got any rest in this foreign city. But they grew accustomed and eventually stopped hearing the traffic. It became like the murmuring of the forest or the rain. Johanna was the first who stopped listening and slept. She had to save her strength, for each new day had to be dealt with as it came along. She was the strongest of them, heavy and well built. It was she who had found jobs and a place to live for all three of them in the new country, and she gave herself credit for that effort. No one knew how hard it had been, least of all Maila and Siiri, who just followed and let things happen. But then they were made of weaker stuff and were born later, when their parents were already worn out. It isn't easy to ask for work and humble yourself in a foreign language that you don't know, while the days go by and the money runs out and you know it's impossible to go home again. Now she and Maila had steady jobs as cleaning women in a factory, and Siiri did the bidding of a housewife in town as a maid. This evening, Johanna was working the night shift.

As she sat and sewed, her thoughts went far back, all the way to the old country, to her father who'd said, "Johanna, now that you're going to America, I'm counting on you to take care of your younger sisters and see that they don't go to the devil. You know better than anyone that they are weak and vacillating, especially Siiri."

"Father," she had answered, "you can rest easy." And he had nodded and gone back to his work.

That was the time of the great emigration to America, when many homesteads were abandoned and animals were sold off for less than they were worth. The crossing was ghastly. When Johanna remembered the storm, she saw the family's *Illustrated Bible* in her mind's eye, with its terrifying pictures of the end of the world when sinners and innocents were cast higgledy-piggledy into darkness to be sorted out on Judgment Day. The family Bible had been very important to her. It would have been a comfort to her here in the new world, but of course a book like that must go to the sons, who carry on the family name. Anyway, the worst part of the trip was that people were ill and vomited and couldn't help themselves. Before it got really bad, she had tried to get Maila and Siiri to sing. Later she settled for holding them by the forehead when they gave in. The stench in the hold grew so strong that she herself was on the verge of letting go, so she wrapped a cloth around her stomach and made it fast with a belt and pretended that she was steering the ship and was responsible for all of them. Then it passed and she grew calm. She was equally calm at Immigration, when their papers weren't in order and the officials wouldn't let them enter. She sat there all day like a rock and wouldn't budge until finally the Americans gave in. That's the way it had been. Now she wrote to Father once a month and gave an account of their lives. Father never answered, because he had other things to do.

When the clothes were mended, Johanna began cooking supper. She closed down her memories and let them rest. Maila was always the first to get home. She was a quiet person and was happiest alone. She had been so even as a child. Now she went in behind the curtain in the corner and changed out of her work clothes into clean ones, then she spread a tablecloth and set the table.

"Why are you setting only two places?" Johanna asked.

"Siiri said to tell you she won't be coming to supper today," Maila answered.

"She could have said so this morning. Is she out with him now again?"

"I don't know," Maila said.

That's the way she was. She wanted to know nothing, take responsibility for nothing, get involved in nothing.

"You should try to keep track of what your sister does," Johanna said when they sat down to eat. "She's younger than you and prettier, and she can be led astray so easily. She tells me nothing, but it'll be me who has to clear up any mess she gets into."

Maila was silent.

"I've got the night shift at the factory," Johanna said. "You'll have to tell me what time she comes home and where she's been. I need to know what's going on. I've mended your clothes and put them in the bottom drawer. Have you rubbed butter on your hands?"

"Yes."

"Good. The skin will crack from all that scrubbing, and then they won't be of any use to anyone."

I know that, Maila thought. After doing the dishes, she lay down on her bed.

"Take a blanket," said her sister. "You shouldn't sleep without something over you."

"I'm not sleeping," Maila said.

Johanna sat by the window and worried about Siiri. If only it hadn't been an Italian. Americans were foreign enough, but she had to go and find herself an Italian, a dark-skinned little good-for-nothing who was shorter than she was. Johanna had seen them down on the street saying good night. Siiri would never have dared bring him up to the room. He had the wrong religion, too. Everything about him was wrong. And when asked, she was snappish and gave flippant, evasive answers and then went and lay on her bed and pretended to sleep. And now Maila lay there the same way, with her face to the wall though it was still early. Suddenly Johanna felt very tired. How am I to cope with them? she thought. I can't even talk to them, they just crawl into their shells. How am I supposed to help them if they don't even hear what I say?

She said, "I've got our folk costumes ready for the Finnish Festival. Now, this time, don't leave the apron at home. Are you asleep?" She waited a moment and said, "We'll have a good time at the Society. Are you asleep or are you awake?"

But Maila didn't answer.

When Johanna came home towards morning, Siiri lay in bed, but she'd thrown her clothes in a pile and her blanket lay on the floor. Johanna picked it up and covered her, and when she bent down over the bed she smelled wine. Siiri lay with her arms thrown over her head like a child, and her round face with its half-open mouth was also that of a child, now, as she slept.

Johanna sat down on the edge of the bed and looked at her sister. She's not pretty, she thought. She has a perfectly ordinary face that no one would look at twice back home. Her legs are too short, and her eyes are very small. But she's young and round and laughs a lot. What am I to do with Siiri, who's throwing herself away without a thought for her future?

She went for a glass of water to put beside the bed and found flowers in the sink, a bouquet in the process of wilting. When she came back with the water, Siiri had turned and her hand lay across her breast. Two wedding rings shone on her finger. God have mercy,

Johanna thought. She hasn't been to work today, she's run off and married her Italian. As quietly as she could, Johanna opened her cot, made it up, and lay down, but she couldn't sleep. She could only think about the future. She knew that the Italian lived with his three brothers in a room somewhere near the harbour and that he wasn't worth having. She knew Siiri had acted out of spite and that she would be unhappy. And she was immeasurably hurt at not having been allowed to help with the arrangements. If misfortune had to occur, they could at least have dressed it up, a party at the Society with coffee and music. Somehow the marriage could have been explained away and given an honourable if pitiful place. Now it was all wrong from beginning to end. Siiri had had no faith in her sister and had not asked for her advice. They could have talked about it. They could have made plans together, and Johanna would have decided what was best for each of them without doing any of them the least harm. For the first time since the hard journey from the old country, Johanna began to cry. Maila no doubt heard her, but she was a coward and pretended to sleep.

When Johanna woke up the next morning, her sisters were up getting ready for work. She got out of bed and sat on the edge of her cot for a while. She was terribly tired.

"Go back to sleep," Siiri said. "You had the night shift. We'll put your coffee under the cosy." Johanna could hear in her voice that she was afraid.

"You're not getting off that easy," Johanna said. "I need to talk to you. But first I'm going to wash my face." She went to the sink and there was complete silence behind her. They're frightened, she thought. They're afraid of me. It was a difficult thought, a thing she had not understood. You take care of people and tend to everything, you're considerate, you struggle and plan, you think you're giving them a good life, and suddenly they turn away from you and are afraid. She washed her face and turned towards the room and said, "I congratulate you on your marriage. We could have had a party at the Society and sent out invitations."

"That's nice of you," Siiri said, looking as if she were hunted by dogs. She had her work satchel and was ready to go.

"Are you leaving right now, this minute?"

"Yes. It's late."

"I think we'd better be off," said Maila, already at the door.

And so they left and nothing further was said. I know, Johanna thought. I know how they run down the stairs. They're relieved, as if they'd gotten away with something, I know how they feel. What is it that's wrong? Why is it like this? They make me so tired, and we have our whole lives ahead of us.

It was a beautiful March day with a sharpness in the air. Spring had come at last.

◆◆◆

That evening, Johanna asked, "Aren't you going to invite him home?"

"He doesn't want to come," Siiri said.

"If he doesn't want to come, it's because you've made him scared of me. What did you tell him?"

"Nothing."

"What does he know about our life?"

"I don't know."

"You don't know," Johanna repeated. "You know nothing, you and Maila. You creep away from everything and say you don't know. It's so easy. And you go and get married, you who thinks everything is easy. You enter into matrimony. Do you know what it means? Do you know what it means to take care of another human being?"

Siiri's answer was cheeky. "Lucio's going to take care of me!"

"Lucio's going to take care of you! That's lovely. He earns nothing, and he'll never be able to give you a home. You can't even consummate your marriage because you don't even own a bed."

Siiri screamed. "Oh! Really! Is that right!? Well, then, give us a bed! Hang up another blanket in some corner and leave us in peace! You've got blankets hung up all over the house anyway, so no one will see the dishpan and the washbowl and everything else you want to hide! You fix everything so fine, so give us our own blanket so we don't have to look at you!"

Johanna didn't answer, but sat very still. Siiri had never before turned on her as if she hated her. It was dreadful to feel this stifled animosity pouring forth in rash words. It was like a powerful blow below the belt.

She made no answer. Siiri stood staring at the floor, then suddenly she sprang into action and ran to the door.

"Take your coat," Johanna said. "It's still cold."

♦♦♦

Siiri was out almost every evening, and when she came home she was surly and silent and went to bed at once.

"Do you talk American to each other?" Maila wondered.

"Yes. What else?"

"But you hardly know any."

"Neither does he."

Siiri was in the habit of not saying Lucio's name at home, not a single time since that first evening. Johanna supposed it was some kind of punishment. "Does he work down at the harbour?" she asked. "Or what does he do?"

"A little of everything. He helps his brother."

"And what does his brother do?"

"I don't know exactly. Business."

"Business," Johanna repeated. "You know what Papa thought about business, and all the trouble he had with the people who do business. And you ought to understand that a person who doesn't dare talk about his work isn't proud of what he does."

"Are you?" Siiri blurted out.

"Yes. I do a good job that I'm not ashamed of." Slowly, Johanna blushed. She looked at her sister and said, "I know I'm red in the face, but if it's a blush of shame, it's not for me but for you. I haven't written to Papa about your marriage, because I can't make things sound better than they are. You'll have to write to him yourself, but show me the letter so I can check your spelling. And the next time you see your Italian, I would ask you to find out what kind of business he's in. Otherwise I'll find out for myself."

Johanna didn't know where Lucio Marandino lived, and she didn't care. She went to the Italian consulate. With the help of her dictionary, she'd composed several questions that required answers, but all they could tell her was that he did odd jobs. On the day they counted their money, Siiri had almost none of her wages left and couldn't contribute to the household pool.

"What did you buy yourself?" Johanna asked her. "You haven't brought home anything new, and you've eaten at home. Don't tell me. I know. You've given your wages to him. He's not earning any money right now. When will it get better?"

"Next week," Siiri said. "He's got something big coming up next week."

♦♦♦

And the following week, Siiri came home with new stockings and a red dress and a necklace that was certainly not made of glass beads. Johanna said nothing. She let Siiri be happy with her presents and asked no questions. If the Italian had found an honourable job, Siiri would have said so herself. But the next day, when the sisters were at work, Johanna took the necklace to a jewellery shop and asked what it was worth. The man behind the counter went into another room, and when he came back he was brusque and wanted to know where she'd got it.

"That's none of your affair," she said. "I want to know what it's worth."

"Is it an heirloom?"

"I don't understand. Is it genuine?"

"The stones are real. Do you want to sell it?"

"No, I just want to know."

He shrugged his shoulders and told her there would be a charge for an appraisal. She didn't understand the words, put the necklace in her purse and went away. But what Johanna had understood – very clearly – was the man's suspicions and the respect in his hands when he touched Siiri's necklace. She was greatly distressed and didn't know what she should do. All through work that day she could think of nothing but the necklace. Mysterious words like "diamonds" and "gemstones" floated through her thoughts. She couldn't tell Siiri that her Italian was a thief. She couldn't tell Siiri she was wearing a fortune around her neck. She couldn't sell the necklace to make life easier for them. She couldn't do a thing. And saying nothing was the same as lying.

By and by, hard times came again for Lucio Marandino, Siiri's wages disappeared, and Johanna was forced to dip into their savings. They never spoke of him. For Siiri, home had become a place where she ate and slept, and she was never happy. She wore the necklace when she went out in the evenings. But one fine day it was gone. Johanna noticed at once. Because Siiri and Maila never told her anything, she was forced to go through their drawers. Belongings reveal a great deal. The necklace was not there. The Italian had taken it back, had sold his gift. Siiri's behaviour would have been different if she had gone and lost it. Now she was merely distant and nonchalant, as if nothing had happened at all.

"Maila," Johanna said, "what has she told you?"

"Nothing."

"Don't you talk to each other? What do you talk about when I'm not home?"

"Oh, nothing much."

Johanna got angry and shouted, "You're like a cow! What do you want? What *is* it? Do you have a good life or don't you?"

"Why are you making such a fuss?" Maila said. "I don't know what you're talking about."

Living together grew very difficult. Sometimes Johanna thought she should give them a little gaiety, but she had no idea how to go about it. Back home, when you felt bad, you went out on the hillside for a while or into the woods, and then you came home again and no one noticed. In a city, you go out and slam the door, or close it terribly quietly, and everyone knows that now she's walking the streets because she's so sick of it all. They know. And, when she comes back, everyone tries to act normal but can't.

Somehow I have to help Siiri, Johanna thought. It can't go on like this. She just sits there and says nothing.

Now the Finnish Society's annual Festival was coming. It was an important event. People made a show of all they'd accomplished during the previous year; everything was noticed and discussed. How could she deliver up her little sister to such judgement? Siiri would arrive with her Italian and they would sit there together, the one with her pale white hair and the other dark and much too small and there would be all those questions about his work and where they lived, all those friendly, stubborn questions that were not meant to help – they were just talk, but dangerous talk that could do much damage. And they had to go to the Society's Festival all three of them – Johanna was on the board.

And so the big day came, the way all things do in time. Siiri wanted to wear the red dress the Italian had given her.

"But this is a Finnish celebration," Johanna said. "The most important one of the year. We wear our folk costumes to honour the old country. Remembering the old country is the only thing of real value we have left."

Suddenly Siiri was beside herself. "You and your memories!" she screamed. "You make all the decisions!" She lost her temper completely and shrieked at her sister. "You can keep your old country! I want to live in the new country and I want to wear my red dress!" And she threw herself on the floor and wept.

Johanna got her onto the bed and put wet towels on her temples. When Siiri had calmed down enough to listen, Johanna said the red dress would be all right. Everything would work out, but Siiri was not to cry and make her face swollen and ugly. After all, she wanted to look pretty for her Italian.

"I don't want to see him," Siiri whispered and began to cry again.

"Maila," said Johanna, "go to the pharmacy and get something soothing. Take the dictionary."

In the evening, they went to the Society. Siiri's face was flushed, and her eyes looked even smaller than usual. Her manner was almost defiant. She spoke quickly and thoughtlessly to everyone they met in the hallway, looking around the whole time, but he hadn't yet arrived. The Society had a space in a school in the eastern part of the city and members were sitting at school desks two by two. The platform was decorated in blue and white, with spruce branches and candles. He came in at the last minute and sat down beside Siiri, who had saved a place for him. Johanna sat behind them with Maila. She looked at his fat little neck with its black locks and thought, This is a bad man. How can he seem so round and childish? The orchestra struck up the national anthem and everyone stood, Lucio Marandino a bit later than the others. Funny, Johanna thought, they're actually round and childish both of them. If they had a child, it would be fat as a piglet. Everyone sat down again. Siiri glanced right and left to see what kind of an impression her Italian was making, and she rested her left hand on the back of the desk in front of her so her wedding rings would show. This was his first time at the Society. From time to time she pressed up against him to show that this man was hers.

"Maila, do you see the way she's carrying on?" Johanna whispered. "Don't speak to her this evening. I've made up my mind for all of us."

Maila stared at her sister Johanna for a long moment, then she looked away and sat quietly as before.

After the lecture and the choir, they all went out into the corridor where coffee and juice were being served. Siiri and her husband did not approach the serving table but stood quietly by the boot rack.

"Wouldn't you like some coffee?" Johanna asked in Finnish. "Shall I get you a cup?"

"No, thank you. I don't care for any."

"If you hide here by the coats, you won't be able to talk to people. It's not often you get to speak your own language outside the four walls of your home."

"I'll talk to Lucio," said Siiri, and she said it as a challenge, loudly, as if she wanted to start an argument.

"You'll be all alone," Johanna replied. "They don't like him." And so it was said and couldn't be taken back.

"It is a very Finnish party," said Lucio Marandino. He spoke bad American. His eyes were like knives. He knew well enough what they were talking about.

"He means it's no fun," Siiri said. "And he's absolutely right. I think your old Society is awful!"

"Now, you're not to disgrace yourself," Johanna said. "You mustn't cry. Here's a handkerchief – go to the lavatory and wait there until you're calm." Siiri took the handkerchief and went. So that's what things had come to, Siiri mocking the Society, the only thing that still bound them to the home they'd left behind. It meant nothing to her that once every month she had the great good fortune to spend an evening in a place where she could speak her own language to any person she met and be understood and be able to say, "Do you remember...?" or "What province are you from and how has life treated you here in the new world...?" No, she had withdrawn from all of them with her Italian, whom she couldn't even talk to, a thief who understood nothing. Johanna turned to him and said in American, "Go away. Leave my sister. You don't have the money for a home. You can't live in our home. No one likes you. It's all wrong."

He answered, "I don't like you. You are an awful person from Finland."

The orchestra began playing folk songs, and people went back and sat down in their places. Siiri sat stiff and straight beside her Italian. Her red dress stood out like a sore thumb in the room. They heard a new lecture, but Johanna had a hard time listening. She was thinking only of the money she had brought with her to buy Siiri's freedom from a life of misery. It was everything they had saved and set aside, a thick purse of black leather, and she had it in her apron pocket. The purse was perfectly safe in her pocket, but her hand kept creeping down to check that it was really still there.

When the Italian got up, she followed him. He went out into the schoolyard to smoke. It was very dark in the yard, but she could see his face in the light from the festival-room windows. They were alone.

"You are not strong," Johanna said. "You're nothing. Leave my sister. No money, no home, we can't help. Go away."

He started speaking Italian, rapidly. When he stopped talking, she went up close to him and said, "You are a thief. I know. I will go to the police."

Lucio Marandino froze. He tried to say something.

"I will go to the police," Johanna shouted.

Then he pulled out a dictionary, gave Johanna his matches, and while she lit one match after another the Italian looked up the words he needed. Finally he said, "Proof. You have no proof."

"But I know," she said.

"You have no proof."

Then Johanna took out the purse and held it out to him. "Count it," she said. He counted the money and stuffed it into his pocket without the slightest trace of shame.

She said, "Now you go away."

For a moment he stood and glared at her. Johanna glared back and thought, Go ahead, hate me. I can take it. You won't get the better of me.

The Italian walked off across the schoolyard, and she went back to the party.

Thereafter they continued to live in their new country, and their fortunes improved. Johanna wrote home every month. "Our lives are good. We have no important news to report."

The Great Journey

"AND WHAT DO WE DO when we get there?" Rosa wondered. "What do two little white mice do when they arrive?"

Elena reached across the bed for her cigarettes. "First of all," she said, "we leave our luggage. Then we're free. It's very early in the morning, and sunny of course. It's warm. We go someplace and have coffee, and we take our time about it. Then we take a street that looks nice and start to look for a hotel."

"A small one," Rosa said. "And you have to do the talking, because that's what big mice do."

"Yes. I'll tell them just two nights, to be on the safe side, so we can move somewhere else if we want. Then we go back for our bags. We'll probably take a taxi to the hotel."

"And what do we do then?"

"We go out and buy fruit. Flowers and lots of fruit – it's all so cheap."

Rosa said, "And we pick out the oranges ourselves. We forgot to do that yesterday when we went to India.

Anyway, it was way too hot. Next time it's my turn to choose the country. Little Mouse chooses."

Elena yawned and pulled the ashtray closer. "And when are we going to travel for real?"

Rosa laughed a little but didn't answer.

"No, look at me. When are we going to travel for real?"

"Sometime....There isn't any rush."

"You think? You're over thirty and you've never travelled. I want your first trip to be with me. I want to show you cities and landscapes and teach you how to look at things in new ways and how to get along in places you don't already know inside out. I want to put some life in you, do you understand?"

"What do you mean, put life in me ...?"

"I want you to stop being an automaton who goes to the bank and then home to Mama and then back to the bank and then home again and who does and thinks only what she's used to doing and thinking. . . You're not curious enough. I want you to wake up!"

Rosa lay on her stomach with her face in a pillow and said nothing.

Elena went on. "Of course, there's your mother. But would it be such a catastrophe if she had to get along without you for a month, a few weeks? Think about it."

"Don't make it hard for me. You know I can't. I just can't. I've told you!"

"Okay," Elena said. "Fine. You can't. We can't even talk about it. Forbidden territory." She turned on the radio and started quietly whistling to the music. Rosa threw off the covers and stood up.

"Are you going home?"

"Yes. It's after eleven."

Elena's room was large and very barren. She didn't like furniture. Nothing on the walls, not a trace of all the stuff that gradually accumulates in a home – no fabrics, no cushions, just a bare room with heaps and piles of books and papers, mostly on the floor. Even the telephone was on the floor, as if Elena had just moved in. In the beginning, Rosa admired the feeling of nonchalant impermanence. Later it struck her as a kind of defiant affectation. It was an insolent room. "But why do you put everything on the floor?" she burst out, pulling on her stockings so quickly she got a run at the ankle.

"I've told you not to pull on your stockings that way," Elena said. "Shall I call you a taxi?"

"No. I'll walk."

"I thought we could have some tea. It's raining. Little Mouse doesn't have a raincoat. Take mine."

"I'm fine the way I am. I don't need a thing."

"Well, tomorrow, then. Are you coming tomorrow?"

"I don't know," Rosa said. "I don't know about tomorrow. Maybe I'll call."

Elena wound her clock, her straight dark hair falling down over her face. "Okay," she said. "Do what you like."

♦♦♦

She went home and opened the door as carefully as she could, very slowly. She extracted the key and stood silently in the dark hall. One time, she ran into her father out on the stairs; he'd taken off his shoes and was holding them in one hand. But it didn't help much. He knocked down some hangers, he always did when he was trying to be quiet. Anyway – he knew perfectly well that Mama was lying awake.

They'd given his clothes to the Salvation Army, all of them. That was a long time ago now.

The lock closed with a little click. She let her coat slip to the floor, removed her shoes and put them down without a sound.

"Rosa, my dear," Mama said. "I put out a plate of food for you in the kitchen. Did you have a nice time?"

"Very nice. But you really didn't need to ... Did I wake you?"

"No, no. Not at all."

Rosa stared into the warm darkness of the bedroom. "You're not in pain?"

"No, I'm just fine. I read for a long time. That Margaret Millar is wonderful. Psychological, you know; not just the murder itself and the police work ... Very entertaining. You'll see. Do you think you could get me some more of hers?"

"I'll get you some more of them," Rosa said and went out to the kitchen. She turned on the ceiling light and looked at her sandwiches. Sausage, cheese, marmalade, beer and cigarettes. And a vase of flowers. She sat down at the table but didn't feel like eating. I'll get some more Millars. Monday after work. Tomorrow I'll go get tickets for that film. Or else I'll stay home all evening. She didn't ask who I was out with; she hasn't asked for a long time.

I'm tired. I'm terribly tired. I don't feel well ... She put the sandwiches in the ice box and turned out the light. Mama was quiet while her daughter undressed and went to bed. Only then did she say, as she always did, "Good night, darling daughter." And Rosa answered, "Good night, dear mother." It was what they always said.

♦♦♦

Sunday. Rosa's mother braided her white hair into two small tails that she knotted together at the back of her neck. She sat very straight. Her book was propped against the coffee maker, and every time she turned a page she secured it with a hairpin. She held the hairpins in her mouth as usual, an old, tightly pursed and wrinkled mouth. She never wore a dressing gown but dressed as soon as she got up, resting a little after the corset and the stockings, then continued with her hair.

Rosa often said, "Mama could sit on her hair when she was young. And it's still the prettiest hair I've ever seen." And Elena replied, "I know. Everything she has is the prettiest you've ever seen. Perfect. Everything she has and does and says is perfect." And Rosa, "You're jealous! You're being unfair. She does whatever she can to make me feel free." "Funny," said Elena slowly. "It's so funny that you don't *feel* free. And rather tiresome for us."

In the beginning, Elena had come home to tea, to dinner. They might go to a movie, all three of them, and Elena would take Mama by the arm and support her as she walked. "I feel so safe," said Mama and laughed. "You take me in tow like a man." That evening she said, "It's so nice you've found such a good friend. A really nice person you can depend on."

But it was some time now since Elena's last visit.

As Mama sat resting after knotting her hair, she wondered out loud how Elena was doing these days.

"Good," Rosa said. "She's got a lot of work at the paper just now."

Mama went back to bed, pulled the covers up tight and opened the big atlas. "Rosa, would you mind?" she said. "I've mislaid them again somewhere. I think they're in the bathroom." Rosa went to find the glasses and Mama said, "You're an angel. I ought to have them on a chain around my neck, but it looks so silly." And she rested the atlas on her knees and started reading along the coastline. Today it was South America.

It would soon be too late for Mama's great journey. She'd been planning it for twenty years – no, longer, right from the beginning, in the early days, when the promises were made and detailed in the nursery along with big hugs. "I'll take you with me. I'll steal you away from Papa. We'll go to the jungle or out on the Mediterranean ... I'll build you a castle where you can be the queen." And they told each other what the castle would look like both outside and in. They took turns furnishing each room, but they always did the throne room together.

The question of a trip had come up again from time to time as the years went by, but there is so much that never gets done. And then there was Papa, of course.

Rosa stood at the window. Without turning around, she asked, "Where would you go if you could choose?"

"Maybe to Gafsa."

"Gafsa? Where's that?"

"North Africa. A place called Gafsa."

"But Mama, why there of all places?"

Mama laughed, her own mysterious laugh that was almost an amused giggle. "It sounds nice. I don't really know. . . It occurred to me."

"But do you really want to go there in particular?"

"Don't look so concerned," Mama said. "I don't need to go anywhere."

"But still, you do think it would be fun."

"Of course. Of course it would be fun."

Rosa compressed her lips. She didn't see the empty Sunday streets, she was looking inwards and backwards to that confusing time when all of a sudden Mama no longer wanted to make decisions or take responsibility. Everything had suddenly lost its framework; there was nothing to hold on to. Mama simply dodged, did not want to decide, not give advice, and if you pressed her she made a little face and left the room. "I'm sure you know best," she'd say. Or "It's hard to tell." Or nothing at all and change the subject. It was frighteningly unlike her. "It scares me," Rosa said one evening and Elena shrugged her shoulders and said, "Naturally. Of course you're frightened. Here she's gone her whole life and told you what to do and think and wish for, and arranged everything for you until you can't do a thing on your own or have a thought of your own in your own head. And then all at once she gets old and retires and your father goes and dies. And she lets go. Don't you get it? Now it's your turn. It's like the changing of the guard, and she's absolutely right. It happens all the time, it's natural." She studied Rosa's narrow uncertain face with its anxious mouth and added, brutally, "Try to get it through our head that your queen no longer has what it takes to make decisions." And, more gently, "Come here. Don't look like that. I want you to be free and smell the breeze. Forget her for a while." And Rosa drew back and struck. "Oh. And so now you're going to be the queen, right?"

"Dear God," Elena said. "These older daughters and their mothers! I can't get free of them. You're all so tough and petrified and hopeless."

And Rosa wept and was comforted.

♦♦♦

She had been uneasy the first time she brought Elena home. But it had gone well right from the start. Elena got Mama to be funny, absolutely playful. She managed to get her telling stories in a completely new way. They had laughed a lot. Rosa was enormously relieved, breathless with relief and gratitude. And afterwards when Elena had gone, Mama went on talking about things that had happened long ago, but not the stories her daughter had heard so many times before. Suddenly her stories had colour – the encounters and journeys, the disappointments and surprises at work and in love – they had all become convincing and vivid. It was Elena that had brought them to life. Elena took Mama the right way. She found her amusing, showed her a kind of casual tenderness and smiled at her in a way that suggested tacit understanding. Elena was a magician who could pull anything at all from her hat. When she felt like it. But now she'd put her hat on the shelf and had stopped coming.

"It's better I stay away," Elena said. "Anyway, how much does she know?"

"Nothing. She knows nothing about such things. But she's disappointed that you never come."

Elena shrugged her shoulders and said she'd run through her entire register and didn't like to repeat herself. And the last time she'd come had been awkward. Rosa remembered. They'd sat on the sofa watching TV, and when the programme ended they sat where they were, close together, and suddenly the silence grew compact and alien. It had nothing to do with the programme, a rather conventional documentary about marsh birds. Elena straightened up, and behind Mama's back she felt for Rosa's hand. Rosa pulled it away. So Elena put her hand on Mama's shoulder. "Birds," she said slowly. "A big marsh no one ever visits, mile after mile of water and reeds, and birds we know nothing about, that have nothing to do with us ... Isn't it remarkable? I mean, there they are, the whole time, and we leave them in peace ..."

Mama sat still without saying a word. Then she stood up and said, "You know what? You're electric. Your hands are electric." And she laughed in her peculiar way – giggled. Rosa felt herself blushing, and she looked at the other two, Elena leaning back in the sofa with a smile, Mama standing there looking back at her over her shoulder. It was nothing, nothing at all, just a very great tension. A little while later, Elena went home.

◆◆◆

I must give Mama her journey. I must hurry, because time is running out. I must find the one best place, a place that is both restful and exciting, where it's beautiful and warm, far enough away to be a real journey but not too far, in case she gets sick. I need to make reservations early and try to get time off from the bank, and it mustn't be too hot, I need to find out about the climate ... The train will be too strenuous, and flying is dangerous for old people; they can have a stroke when the plane descends. If it descends too fast ...

◆◆◆

"Elena, have you ever been to a place called Gafsa?"

"God forbid. What's it supposed to be? Is that where she wants go to?"

"She doesn't really know ... She said something about a place in North Africa called Gafsa."

"Poor Little Mouse," Elena said. "What's up? Are you trying to get me to plan your trip? Shall I scare you? I've applied for a travel grant, and it looks like I might get it." Her gaze was fixed steadily on Rosa. Finally she said,

"Your face is falling. There's nothing in the world makes you so little and grey as the need to choose and decide."

"But we've got time – there's plenty of time," Rosa mumbled.

Elena answered, "Don't be too sure." And then she spoke of other things entirely, lightly, heedlessly. She encapsulated the danger and pushed it away, presented it to her friend. A ruthless gift.

♦♦♦

Now, this empty late winter day, Mama lay reading her way along the coast of South America. Florianopolis, she read. Rio Grande. San Pedro. Montevideo. The Rio de la Plata is right here ... San Antonio ... She whispered their names.

"Listen," Rosa said. "What do you know about those places? Nothing. Nothing at all. Don't you have any desire to read about them, find out about them? Why don't you ever want travel books? Only murder mysteries?" Her voice was mean, she could hear it herself.

"I don't really know," Mama said. "They're such pretty names ...Maybe I just like to imagine what they look like. And murder mysteries ... You know, they're so relaxing. And it amuses me trying to figure out who the murderer is before the author does the summing up in the library." She giggled and added, "But sometimes I peek at the end. It's unbelievable the trouble they take to fool the reader. Mostly pretty contrived. But I'm on to them. Bahia. We could go to Bahia."

And, like a billowing sea, love for her mother swept over her. She was utterly helpless in its grip. She said, "We'll travel. We'll go somewhere, we'll go now. But are you really sure Gafsa is where you want to go?"

Mama took off her glasses and smiled. "Rosa," she said, "you shouldn't worry so much. Come here. Are you all alone in the woods?"

They played their game. With her face against her mother's throat, as close as she could come. "Yes, I'm all alone in the woods."

"And does someone find you?"

"Yes, someone finds me."

Hands caressed the back of her neck, and suddenly the hands were unbearable. She tore herself loose and her temper flared, but she said nothing. Mama raised the atlas again and turned a little towards the wall.

They ate at two o'clock: Sunday chicken with vegetables.

◆◆◆

She went down to the corner to call. "Can I come over?"

"Come ahead," Elena said. "But I'm warning you, I'm in a bad mood. You know how I loathe Sundays."

Every time Rosa walked into the bare, serious room, she felt a thrill of expectation, of unease. It was like daring to enter a no-man's-land where you might encounter anything at all. The room was empty.

"Hi," Elena said from the kitchen door. She held two glasses in her hand. "I thought we might need a drink. Why do you have your coat on? Are you cold?"

"It is a little chilly. I'll take it off in a minute." Rosa took her glass and sat down.

"Well, has Little Mouse been thinking?"

"About what?"

"Oh, nothing," Elena said. "Here's to the great journey."

Rosa drank without a word.

"Sitting there like that," Elena went on, "on the edge of your chair and with your coat on, you look like something at a railway station. When does the train leave? Or are you flying?" She threw herself on the bed and closed her eyes. "Sundays," she said. "I despise them. Have you got any cigarettes?"

Rosa threw her cigarette pack and threw it hard. It hit Elena in the face.

"Aha," said Elena without moving. "So the Mouse has a temper. Well, how about the lighter. Try again."

"You know perfectly well," Rosa shouted. "You know perfectly well that I can't go off and leave her alone! It's out of the question. There's nothing more to say on the subject. There's no one who can stay with her while I'm gone. And I can't leave her with a stranger!"

"Fine, fine," Elena said. "Okay. I get it. She can't have a stranger in the house. She can only have you. Clear as a bell."

Rosa got up. "I'm going now," she said, and waited. Elena lay where she was and stared at the ceiling with an unlit cigarette between her lips. Someone was playing the piano somewhere in the building – they could hear it very faintly. Whoever it was always played on Sundays and always operetta tunes. Rosa walked over to the bed and lit her lighter. "I'm going now," she repeated. Elena raised her head. Resting on her elbow, she took the light. "Do as you like," she said. "It isn't much fun around here."

"Shall I refill your glass?" Rosa asked.

"Yes, thanks."

She took the glass out to the kitchen. There were no curtains, no furniture, everything was simply white. Standing in the middle of the room, Rosa felt suddenly sick to her stomach with a sense of impending catastrophe. Something awful was happening, something unavoidable. I can't deal with this ... No one could deal with this. But I haven't promised anything, absolutely nothing, it was just playing, the way people play with words. Elena must have understood that I wasn't serious ... I'm not going anywhere! Not with anyone ...

"What's the matter with you," Elena said, standing beside her.

"I don't feel well. I'm going to throw up."

"Here's the slops," Elena said. "Lean forward. Try. Stick your finger down your throat." Her strong hands held Rosa's forehead and she said, "Do as I say. Get rid of it so I can talk to you."

Afterwards she said, "Sit down here. Are you afraid of me?"

"I'm afraid of disappointing you."

"The only thing you're really afraid of", Elena said, "is that it's your fault. Everything's been your fault since the day you were born, and that's why no one can ever be happy with you. I don't want to travel with you as long as you think you ought to be somewhere else. And neither does your mother."

Rosa said, "She doesn't know what it's like for me."

"Of course she does. She's not dumb. She tries as best she can to set you free, but you stick to her like glue and roll yourself in your bad conscience. What is it you want?"

Rosa didn't answer.

"I know," Elena said. "You'd really like to travel with both of us, and however hopeless that trip turned out to be, you'd be happy because it wasn't your fault. Am I right? You'd be content."

"But we can't," Rosa whispered.

"No. We can't." Elena walked back and forth across the kitchen. Finally she stopped behind Rosa, put her hands on her shoulders, and asked, "What is it you want most of all, right now. Think about it."

"I don't know."

"You don't know. Then I'll tell you what you want. You want to fly to the Canary Islands with your mama. It's warm and just exotic enough. There are doctors. And tomorrow you're going to go and book tickets and a hotel."

Rosa said, "But flying ..."

"They descend very gently – she'll be fine. It's all decided. You don't need to think about it any more – you don't need to make any decisions about anything. I've decided."

Rosa turned around on her chair and looked at Elena. "But what about you?" she said.

"We'll see. Right at the moment, I don't have the strength to deal with you. And now you should go home. Tell her about the trip." Elena watched the face in front of her smooth over in immense relief and become almost beautiful. She stepped back and said, "Forget about being grateful. You're a mouse. Now you can dance on the table for a while. But at least be happy while you're dancing."

"And later?" Rosa shouted. "Afterwards?"

"I don't know," Elena answered. "How can we know how it's going to be for us? Some queens reign for a very long time."

Also by Tove Jansson

THE SUMMER BOOK

"The Summer Book is a marvellously uplifting read, full of gentle humour and wisdom." Justine Picardie, *Daily Telegraph*

An elderly artist and her six-year-old grand-daughter while away a summer together on a tiny island in the gulf of Finland. As the two learn to adjust to each other's fears, whims and yearnings, a fierce yet understated love emerges – one that encompasses not only the summer inhabitants but the very island itself.

Written in a clear, unsentimental style, full of brusque humour, and wisdom, *The Summer Book* is a profoundly life-affirming story. Tove Jansson captured much of her own life and spirit in the book, which was her favourite of her adult novels. This edition has a foreword by Esther Freud.

A WINTER BOOK

"As smooth and odd and beautiful as sea-worn driftwood, as full of light and air as the Nordic summer. We are lucky to have these stories collected at last." Philip Pullman

A Winter Book features thirteen stories from Tove Jansson's first book for adults, *The Sculptor's Daughter* (1968) along with seven of her most cherished later stories (from 1971 to 1996). Drawn from youth and older age, this selection by Ali Smith provides a thrilling showcase of the great Finnish writer's prose, scattered with insights and home truths. It is introduced by Ali Smith, and there are afterwords by Philip Pullman, Esther Freud and Frank Cottrell Boyce.

FAIR PLAY

"So what can happen when Tove Jansson turns her attention to her own favourite subjects, love and work, in the form of this novel about two women, lifelong partners and friends? Expect something philosophically calm – and discreetly radical. At first sight it looks autobiographical. Like everything Jansson wrote, it's much more than it seems … *Fair Play* is very fine art." From Ali Smith's introduction

What mattered most to Tove Jansson, she explained in her eighties, was work and love, a sentiment she echoes in this tender and original novel. *Fair Play* portrays a love between two older women, a writer and artist, as they work side-by-side in their Helsinki studios, travel together and share summers on a remote island. In the generosity and respect they show each other and the many small shifts they make to accommodate each other's creativity we are shown a relationship both heartening and truly progressive.

THE TRUE DECEIVER

"I loved this book. It's cool in both senses of the word, understated yet exciting … the characters still haunt me." Ruth Rendell

In the deep winter snows of a Swedish hamlet, a strange young woman fakes a break-in at the house of an elderly artist in order to persuade her that she needs companionship. But what does she hope to gain by doing this? And who ultimately is deceiving whom? In this portrayal of two women encircling each other with truth and lies, nothing can be taken for granted. By the time the snow thaws, both their lives will have changed irrevocably.

TRAVELLING LIGHT

"Jansson's prose is wondrous: it is clean, deliberate; an aesthetic so certain of itself it's breathtaking." Kirsty Gunn, *Daily Telegraph*

Travelling Light takes us into new Tove Jansson territory. A professor arrives in a beautiful Spanish village only to find that her host has left and she must cope with fractious neighbours alone; a holiday on a Finnish Island is thrown into disarray by an oddly intrusive child; an artist returns from abroad to discover that her past has been eerily usurped. With the deceptively light prose that is her hallmark, Tove Jansson reveals to us the precariousness of a journey – the unease we feel at being placed outside of our millieu, the restlessness and shadows that intrude upon a summer.

Other Tove Jansson titles
published by Sort Of Books

Novels and stories

The Summer Book
A Winter Book
Fair Play
The True Deceiver
Travelling Light

Picture books for children

The Book about Moomin, Mymble and Little My
Who Will Comfort Toffle?
The Dangerous Journey

Also published as an App

The Book about Moomin, Mymble and Little My